How *Not* To Marry A Millionaire:

1. Drive to his lodge in the middle of the night to break off your engagement.

2. Find yourself stranded at his place with nothing but the wet clothes on your back.

3. Resolve to tell him you're through right then and there.

4. Lose your nerve.

5. Kiss him.

6. Ask him to make love to you.

7. Hate him for acting like a gentleman.

8. Break off your engagement.

9. Kiss him again.

10. Thank him for forgetting how to be a gentleman....

Dear Reader,

The romance-writing community is a small one. After a time you count many authors as friends or friends of friends. Not many degrees separate each one of us.

It's a fabulous perk of the job, and I'm always thrilled to meet and get to know other authors because so often I already know their work. (Writers are the most voracious of readers, or at least this one is!) So when a friend mentioned coming up with a series for the Desire line, it didn't take long for us to gather together other friends. No surprise that we ended up writing about friends, too!

Okay, yes, they're male friends, and rich, and sexy… but boy did our group have fun dreaming up their group. I hope you'll have fun with them, too. My hero, Luke Barton, is like all the other Samurai. Rich and sexy. But he's also ruthless and driven, and hurting for reasons that seem to come together when a blonde shows up on the doorstep in the rain….

I hope you enjoy watching a hard man find the tenderness inside him. It's been a pleasure to tell his story.

Best,

Christie Ridgway

CHRISTIE RIDGWAY

HIS
FORBIDDEN
FIANCÉE

Silhouette® Desire

Published by Silhouette Books
America's Publisher of Contemporary Romance

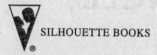 SILHOUETTE BOOKS

ISBN-13: 978-0-373-76791-5
ISBN-10:   0-373-76791-9

HIS FORBIDDEN FIANCÉE

Visit Silhouette Books at www.eHarlequin.com

Printed in U.S.A.

CHRISTIE RIDGWAY

is a *USA TODAY* bestselling author who has been writing contemporary romance for over a decade. Her love of romances began when she spent all her babysitting money on novels from Harlequin Books, and she's still happiest when reading a story with a guaranteed happy-ever-after.

A native Californian, she has a busy family life (husband, two sons, yellow labrador, two turtles, a tortoise, four parakeets, two crawdads, two bearded dragon lizards and assorted fish) and lives in the "corner house," which is a natural gathering place for the neighborhood kids (all boys). She loves the chaos—that is, until the feeder-crickets escape captivity. Then her office is her retreat, and her stories are her escape.

For Elizabeth Bevarly, Maureen Child,
Susan Crosby, Anna DePalo and Susan Mallery.
Thanks for making this project so much fun!

One

The only thing the first-class-all-the-way log house lacked was a sexy female in the master bedroom's quilt-covered sleigh bed. Make that a naked sexy female. Blond. Curvy.

Make that lots of curves.

Coat hangers with legs didn't interest Luke Barton. He liked his women built for pleasure. His pleasure.

"Did you say something, Mr. Barton?"

He started, then tore his gaze from the decadent bed to frown at the caretaker who was showing him through the home that was his for the next month. Had he been talking out loud? Luke shoved his hands in his pockets and tried out a noncommittal smile before trailing the woman toward the adjoining bathroom.

She was attractive enough, he supposed, and somewhere in her twenties as well as sort of blondish, but it wasn't her who had sparked his imagination. It was that luxurious bed, he decided, glancing back at it over his shoulder. That quilt-covered bed with a mattress wide enough to rival the sizable slice of Lake Tahoe that he could see through the room's tall windows.

There was a stone fireplace near the bed's carved footboard with wood neatly laid inside and Luke could imagine the logs burning brightly, licking golden color along the naked, fair flesh of his fantasy woman. He'd follow suit with his tongue, tasting her warm—

"Mr. Barton?"

His attention jolted to the caretaker again and he realized he was standing, frozen, in the middle of the room. "Call me Luke," he said.

"What?" The caretaker frowned. "We were expecting Matthias Barton this month."

Perplexed, Luke stared at her for a moment. Matthias?

Oh. *Matthias*. Matt. That luxurious decadent bed was making him forget everything. It wasn't often that Luke Barton forgot his bastard of a twin brother, Matt. And it was never that he did his bastard of a brother a favor.

Except for now.

Damn Matt.

When his assistant had called Luke's assistant he'd wished like hell he could have turned the cheating, thieving SOB down flat. *"Your brother has to take care of some unexpected business and he wants to know if you'll switch months with him,"* Elaine had imparted, as if it wasn't damn strange that identical siblings refused to speak to each other.

But for once, Luke had been unable to refuse his brother's request.

"I'm sorry. I meant to mention it right away," Luke told the caretaker. Apparently she hadn't noticed the cryptic note Nathan left behind had been addressed to him. "Something came up and my brother and I had to trade months." The ol' twin switcheroo.

"Oh, I suppose that's all right," the woman replied, then gestured him forward. "So, as I was saying, Luke, you must spend the next month in the lodge in order to fulfill the requirements of Hunter's will. Your friend Nathan was here last month and your brother Matthias will then take your place in the fifth month."

Luke knew all that. A while back, letters had been received by each of the remaining "Seven Samurai" as they'd called themselves in college. The six had lost touch after the death of Hunter Palmer and graduation, but with the arrival of those letters they'd been reminded of the promise they'd once made to one another as they closed in on getting their diplomas. Though they were from families of distinction and wealth, they'd been determined to each make their own mark on the world. In ten years, they'd vowed.

Over a table filled with empty beer bottles they'd pledged to build a lodge on the shores of Lake Tahoe and in ten years, each of them would take the place for a month. At the end of the seventh month, the plan had been that they'd all come together for a celebration of their friendship and the successes they'd achieved.

But after Hunter's illness and subsequent death, that dream had died with him.

Though apparently not for Hunter. Even aware he wouldn't be there to share it with them, he'd made arrangements for a lodge to be built at the lake. The letters he'd written to each of the friends said that he expected them to honor the vow they'd taken all those years ago.

The caretaker stepped aside as they reached another arched doorway. "And here's the master bathroom."

As Luke stepped inside, the fantasy blond popped back into his thoughts. The light of a fire was tracing her skin again, all that pretty, pretty skin, as she lowered herself into the deep porcelain tub that was surrounded by slate and butted up against yet another fireplace. The ends of her hair darkened as they swished against her wet shoulders. Bubbles played peekaboo with her rosy nipples.

"Do you think you'll be comfortable here?"

Sidetracked again by his enticing little vision, Luke was jolted once more by the sound of the caretaker's voice.

Damn! What was the matter with him? he wondered, firmly banishing the distracting beauty splashing in his suddenly sex-obsessed brain.

"I'll be just fine here, thank you." Even though he was going to be "just fine" three months early, all for the sake of his brother.

He must have been scowling at the thought, because the woman's eyebrows rose. "Is something wrong?"

"No. Not at all." There was no reason to expose the family laundry to a stranger. "I guess I'm just thinking of…of Hunter."

The woman's gaze dropped. "I'm sorry." The toe of

her sensible black shoe appeared to fascinate her. "I think…I think he intended this as a nice gesture."

"Hunter Palmer was a very nice man." The best of the seven of them. The very best. Luke let himself remember Hunter's wide grin, his infectious laugh, the way he could rally their group to do anything from nailing all the furniture in the freshman-dorm rec room to the ceiling to organizing a charity three-man basketball tournament senior year.

Hunter had been part of Luke's squad. They'd won the whole shebang, too. What a team they'd made, Hunter and Luke…and Matt.

In those days, like never before and never since, Luke and Matt had played on the same side.

But it was Hunter who Luke had been thinking of when he'd agreed to take his brother's place for the next month. Their dead friend's last request had been for the six other men to spend time at the lodge he'd built. If they fulfilled his request, then twenty million dollars and the lodge itself would be turned over to the town of Hunter's Landing, here on the shores of Lake Tahoe.

Luke wasn't going to be the reason that didn't happen, no matter how he felt about his brother.

So he followed the caretaker through the rest of the rooms, keeping his mind off the fantasy blond by thinking of the twin switcheroo and how he was replacing Matt Barton, #1 bastard. He spent little time looking on the framed Samurai photos mounted in the second-floor hallway. If he were really playing the part of Matt, Luke thought, it would mean keeping his tie knotted tight, his smiles as cold as Sierra snow, and his mind open to how he could take advantage of any situation without regard to kith, kin or even common decency.

That was how his brother operated.

Finally the caretaker gave him the ornate keychain that contained the house key and departed, leaving Luke alone inside the big house with only his grim thoughts for company. The place was quiet and absent of any signs of Nathan Barrister—who had been staying here the month before—unless you counted the hastily written note Luke had found from him. But Nathan hadn't gone far. He'd fallen for the mayor of Hunter's Landing, Keira Sanders, and now they were flitting between the Tahoe town and sun-filled Barbados, where his old friend was presumably mixing business with pleasure.

Jacket and tie discarded, Luke found a beer in the overstocked fridge and settled himself by the window of the great room. Through the trees was another spectacular view of the lake. It wasn't its famous clear-blue at the moment, not only because it was settling into evening, but also because gray clouds were gathering overhead.

Dark clouds that reflected Luke's mood.

What the hell was he going to do with himself for a month?

Nathan had done okay here, apparently. His note said it wasn't "exactly the black hole I thought" and he'd occupied himself by jumping into a full-on love affair. Luke didn't wish that potential quagmire on himself, though a visit from that blond sweetheart of his imagination might make the month pass just a little bit faster. It was too damn bad she couldn't stroll out of his fantasies and straight into this room.

Yes, that would make the thirty days more interesting.

Except it wasn't going to happen unless Matt had invited someone to join him here. And even if that were the case, blond sweethearts just weren't Matt's type. Being identical twins didn't mean they had identical taste when it came to women.

Luke hooked his heels around a nearby ottoman and dragged it closer as the first drops of what appeared to be a heavy spring rain started to hit the windows and roll down like tears. Yeah, he'd be crying, too, if the vision from his daydream showed up on his doorstep looking for Matt.

Though he shouldn't rule that out, come to think of it. His brother might set up just such a thing to shake Luke's cage. Matt ruined Luke's life any chance he got.

To be fair—unlike his brother—Luke had to admit that it was their father, Samuel Sullivan Barton, who had sowed the seeds of their ugly rivalry. He'd run their childhood like an endless season of *The Apprentice,* with himself playing Donald Trump, constantly orchestrating cutthroat competitions between his two sons.

Their enmity had abated in college. But after Hunter had died, so had their father, and he'd left behind one last contest that rekindled his sons' competitive fire. Whichever twin made a million dollars first would win the family holdings. Both of them had separately gone to work on developing wireless technology—Luke doing it hands-on, using his engineering degree, while Matt tapped into his undeniable business acumen to hire someone to work with him.

When it came to any kind of gadgetry, his brother

was all thumbs. But when it came to building a successful team, Matt was a master.

Of course, that time he'd ensured his mastery by bribing a supplier and knocking Luke right out of the running. Matt had made the first mil and won all the family assets, to boot.

Luke hadn't spoken to his brother since, though he'd gone on to do a damn fine job with his own company—a meaner and leaner version of what Matt continued to build upon with the Barton family wealth behind him. That was Luke in a nutshell these days: a leaner—okay, maybe by only a pound or two—but definitely meaner version of his brother Matt.

Working his ass off had a way of doing that to a man, Luke thought. And maybe bitterness, too. He couldn't deny it.

The rain was really coming down now, and the house took on a chill. He got up and lit the fire laid in the great room's massive fireplace—it took up one huge stone wall—and the flames set him thinking about his blond again.

When he got back to his own condo in the San Francisco Bay Area he was going to have to make a few phone calls, apparently. This fantasy woman was a new fixation for him. Work usually was his only obsession—work and finding some way to pay back his brother at some future date—so his sex life was more sporadic than people believed. It looked as if he needed to be paying more attention to his bodily needs, though.

Or maybe the blame rested on this house, he thought. Or the fireplaces. *That bed.*

The blond continued insinuating herself into his thoughts. He could practically smell her now. Her scent was like rain—clean, cool rain—and he'd sip the drops off her mouth, her neck, her collarbone.

Closing his eyes, he rested his head against the back of the chair. As his fantasy played on, his heart started to hammer.

Except that it wasn't his heart.

His eyes popped open. He stared out the windows, trying to determine if the pouring rain or the waving trees were causing the loud drumming.

He decided it was neither one.

Luke set his beer down and rose, following the noise to the front door. Who the hell would be here now and in this spring deluge?

He jerked open the door. As he took in the dark shadow of a figure on the porch, a chilly blast of wind and a spray of rain wafted over him. Suppressing a shiver, he fumbled for the light switches. Brightness blazed over the porch and in the foyer.

The shadowy figure became a woman.

Her white blouse was plastered to her body. Wet denim clung to her thighs.

She raised a hand to her hair and tried fluffing the drenched stuff. A few locks gamely sprung from straight strands into bedraggled curls that hinted at gold.

Luke looked back at her clothes again.

More accurately, he looked at the curves cupped by all that wet cloth.

Her nipples were hard buds topping spectacular breasts.

Even from the front he could surmise she had a round backside, too, just the way he liked it.

She was exactly how he liked it.

Bemused, he continued to stare at her as he tried figuring out what combination of beer, rain and rampant fantasy had brought such a sight to his front door.

Could she possibly be real? And if so, whom did he have to thank for such a surprising gift?

She frowned at him. Her lips were generously pillowed, too. "Matthias, aren't you going to invite your fiancée in?"

Fiancée? Matthias?

Luke spent a few more long moments staring at the wet blonde on his doorstep. When another cold blast of air and rain slapped him, he blinked and finally stepped back to let his brother's fiancée inside.

As she moved forward, questions circled in his mind. Was this some joke? That trick he hadn't put past his brother? Or could Matt really be engaged? If so, it was news to Luke. He'd thought his brother was the same kind of workaholic confirmed bachelor he was. And when had Matt's taste turned to blondes?

Inside, with the door shut behind her, the young woman wrapped her arms around herself and licked her bottom lip in what seemed a nervous gesture. "I, um, know you weren't expecting me. It was sort of an—an impulse."

"Oh?"

"Yes. I jumped in my car and before long I was almost here. Then it started pouring rain and now…" Her voice drifted off and she shrugged, her gaze going to her feet. "And now I'm dripping all over this beautiful carpet."

She was right. She was as wet as his bathtub fantasy, and probably cold, too. He gestured up the stairs toward the great room and its crackling fire. "Let's get you warmed up and dried off."

He tried to be a gentleman and keep his gaze above her neck as she preceded him into the other room but, hell, he knew he was no gentleman. So he confirmed what he'd already suspected by running his gaze from her nape to her heels. She was just his type.

Except she was his brother's fiancée. Or was she? It could still be a trick…

Stopping in front of the roaring fire, she faced him again. Another rush of words spilled out, giving him the idea that she chattered when she was anxious. "My mother would kill me if she knew I came up here. 'Lauren,' she'd say in that disapproving tone of hers, 'is this another one of your Bad Ideas?' That's just how she says it, with capitals. Capital *B*, Bad. Capital *I*, Ideas. 'Another one of Lauren's Bad Ideas.'" A nervous laugh escaped before her hands came up to try to suppress it.

Lauren. Her name was Lauren. It didn't ring any bells, but Luke didn't keep tabs on Matt's social life. Maybe he should, if his brother was really going around snatching up just the sort of women that Luke liked. For God's sake, Matt shouldn't be allowed to have everything Luke wanted.

She shivered and he spotted a wool throw draped over a nearby chair. He grabbed for it then brought it to her. As she took it from his hand, she looked up at him, all big, blue eyes. Her pink tongue darted out to wet that pouty lower lip.

"You've got to be wondering why I'm here, Matthias."

"I'm not—" Matthias. But something made him hold that last word back. He ran his hand through his hair, buying himself some time. "I guess I am a little surprised to see you."

She gave another small laugh and then turned toward the fire. "This whole engagement thing has been a little surprising, don't you agree?"

"Yeah." He could be honest about that, anyway. "I suppose so."

She continued to study the fire. "I mean, we don't know each other that well, right? You've worked with my father and Conover Industries for years, of course…"

Hell, Luke thought. She was Conover's kid. Ralph Conover's daughter. Ralph Conover, who'd been the first to cozy up to Matt after he'd cheated Luke out of his fair chance to win the Barton family holdings.

"…but there's the fact that we haven't talked that much or ever really been…um, alone together."

What? Luke stared at the back of her head and the gold curls that were starting to spring up there. His brother was engaged to marry a woman he'd never been alone with? Luke had a guess to what that was code for and, if he was right, it meant Matt *hadn't* suddenly developed a yen for cute curvy blondes.

Instead, it meant Matt had developed a yen to more tightly cement his relationship with Conover Industries. Luke's mind raced ahead as he imagined all the implications this could have for Eagle Wireless, his own smaller company. With Conover Industries and Barton Limited "married," Eagle could find its own perch in the wireless world very precarious.

God. Damn. It.

Lauren turned toward him again, clutching the throw at her chest. "You haven't said what you think about that, Matthias."

Because Luke hadn't had enough time to think it through completely. He cleared his throat. "I suppose some people would find it a bit odd that we haven't..." Since he didn't know precisely what Matt and Lauren had or hadn't, he let the sentence hang.

"Touched?" she conveniently supplied. "Even kissed, really?" Then color reddened her cheeks. "And we certainly haven't made love."

Staring into her big, blue eyes, suddenly Luke could picture—in vivid detail—doing just that very thing with her. He saw it on his mind's high-def big screen, the two of them making love in that big bathtub upstairs, Lauren's soft, wet thighs wrapped around his hips. Or on that quilt-covered bed, her blond curls spread out against the pillowcase.

Her eyes darkened and he heard a tiny gasp as her breath suddenly caught. Was she reading his thoughts?

Or did she feel that same sharp tug of attraction that he did?

Could she possibly share the images dealing out like X-rated playing cards in his mind?

Blond, curvy Lauren, and Luke, the mean twin.

The cheated twin.

He lifted his hand and trailed one knuckle along the

downy softness of her cheek, wondering if she would taste as sweet as she looked. His fingertip touched the center of her bottom lip and he saw her eyes widen.

Oh, yeah, the message in them made it clear that she felt the attraction, too. And the bit of confusion he could read as well told him she hadn't felt it for Matt.

Luke ran his thumb over her bottom lip this time, moving inside just a little so that he grazed the damp inner surface. She stood frozen before him, trapped between the fire and his touch. In the sudden heavy silence of the room he could hear the light, fast pants of her breath. Color ran high on her cheeks.

God, she was beautiful.

And we certainly haven't made love.

She'd said that, and that's where Luke's brother had slipped up. If she were Luke's, he wouldn't have wasted any time before taking their engagement—even one motivated by business reasons—to a more serious level.

Okay, be honest. He wouldn't have been able to stop himself.

The pulse along her throat was racing, begging him to touch it with his mouth. And now that her hair was starting to dry, he could smell her shampoo, something flowery, but not cloying. It was a fresh smell and he wanted to rub himself against it. He wanted to smell her on his own skin.

Really, it came down to one very simple thing. He wanted his brother's bride-to-be.

"M-Matthias?" she whispered.

Luke didn't flinch at the wrong name. Instead, he tucked a damp curl behind her ear. At the sight of the goose bumps that raced down her neck in response, he smiled, careful to keep the wolfishness out of it.

But he felt wolfish.

Smug, satisfied and ready to eat Goldilocks up in one big bite.

And then he'd want to do it again, this time taking his time to savor every taste.

His hand lingered near her shell of an ear. He'd mixed up his fairy tales, hadn't he? The wolf was Little Red Ridinghood's nemesis, wasn't he? But no matter. Lauren was most certainly Goldilocks and Luke hadn't felt this predatory in a long, long while.

Catching her gaze with his, he grazed his thumb along her velvety cheek.

She released her grip on the wool throw. It fell at her feet as she circled his wrist to pull his hand away from her face. "What do you think you're doing?"

Goldilocks wasn't quite so ready to test out feather mattresses as he'd thought. But that was okay. He needed some time to process all this himself. "Nothing you don't want," he reassured her, stepping back and trying on another smile.

She shivered again.

Frowning, he ran his gaze over her, noting that her wet clothes still clung. He shoved his hands in his pockets to disguise the effect her curves had on him and cleared his throat. "Why don't you take a hot shower? Warm up."

So he could cool down. Think things through. Decide what to do with all the sexual dynamite in the room, especially when they were standing so close to the fire.

Especially when the woman who had walked out of his fantasies was his brother's bride-to-be.

"Take a shower *here?*" She was already shaking her head. "No, no, no. I only came to talk and then—"

"What?" Luke interrupted. "Go back out in that?" He gestured toward the windows and the full-on storm and wilderness-level darkness beyond them. "Now *that* would definitely be a Bad Idea, Lauren."

She made a face. "Oh, thanks for reminding me."

He allowed himself a little grin. "Fair warning, kid. Never show me your weakness. I'll use it against you."

"Kid." She made the face again, though he could see the appellation relaxed her. "I'm twenty-six years old."

"Be a grown-up then. Go upstairs and take a hot shower. Then we'll put your clothes in the dryer, I'll rustle us up some dinner and after that we'll reassess."

Her eyes narrowed. "Reassess what?"

She was a suspicious little thing, but God knows that was sensible of her. He shrugged. "We'll reassess whatever occurs to us." Like whether he should let her know who he really was. Like whether he could let her drive away from him tonight.

After another swift glance at the scene outside the windows, she appeared to make up her mind. "All right." She bent to retrieve the throw.

As she handed it to him on her way toward the stairs, he used it to reel her closer.

"What?" she said, startled. Round blue eyes. Quivering curls.

"We haven't had our hello kiss," he murmured.

Then, curious as to what it might be like, he placed his mouth on top of hers.

At contact, his heart kicked hard inside his chest. Heat flashed across his flesh, burning from scalp to groin.

Lauren had the softest, most pillowy lips he'd ever encountered in thirty-one years of living. Eighteen years of kissing. His biceps were tight as he lifted his hands to cradle her face.

He took a breath in preparation, then touched the tip of his tongue to hers.

Pow.

They both leaped away from the sweet, hot explosion.

She regained her breath first. "I'll...I'll just take that shower," she said, her gaze glued to his face as if she were afraid to turn her back on him.

"Sure, fine, go on up," he managed to get out, when he should have said, *"Run, Goldilocks. Run as far and as fast as you can."*

As if he wouldn't run right after her if she tried.

Two

Lauren Conover stared at her bedraggled reflection in the bathroom mirror, looking for any evidence of the backbone she'd thought she'd found this morning before driving to Lake Tahoe. Instead, all she saw was a wet woman with reddened lips and a confused expression in her eyes.

"You were supposed to walk in and break it off with him immediately," she whispered fiercely to that dazed-looking creature staring back at her. "Nowhere in the plan were you supposed to find him attractive."

But she had! That was the crazy, spine-melting trouble. When the door to the magnificent log house had opened, there stood Matthias Barton, looking as he always had on those few occasions they'd been together. Dark hair, dark eyes, a lean face that she couldn't deny was handsome—and yet, never before had it drawn her.

Then he'd invited her inside and when she'd been looking up at him with the fire at her back she'd felt fire at her front, too. A man-woman kind of fire that made her skin prickle and her heart beat fast.

The kind of fire that a woman might be persuaded to marry for.

And she'd come all this way to tell him it wasn't going to happen.

And it wasn't!

When her mother had plopped a stack of bridal magazines onto the breakfast table that morning, Lauren had looked at them and then at her thirteen-year-old sister's face. Her tough-as-nails tomboy sister who had been giving Lauren grief since the engagement had been announced two weeks before.

"You'd better do something quick," Kaitlyn had said, backing away from the glossy magazines as if they were a tangle of hissing snakes. "Or the next thing you know, Mom will have me in some horrid junior bridesmaid's dress that I'll never, ever forgive you for."

Lauren had known Kaitlyn was right. Her mother's steamroller qualities were exactly why she'd found herself engaged to a man she barely knew in the first place. That is, her mother's steamroller qualities combined with her father's heavy-handed hints about this marriage being good for the family business he always claimed was faltering. As well as Lauren's own embarrassment over her three previous attempts to make it down the aisle.

She'd picked those men herself and the engagements had each ended in disaster.

So it had been hard to disagree with her mother and father that their choice couldn't be any worse, despite Kaitlyn's teenage disgust.

But the sight of those pages and pages of bridal gowns had woken Lauren from the stupor that she'd been suffering since returning home from Paris six months before. Hanging a third now-never-to-be-worn wedding dress in the back of her family's cedar-lined luggage closet had sent her to a colorless, emotionless place where she'd slept too much, watched TV too much and responded almost robot-like to her parents' commands.

Until glimpsing that tulled and tiara-ed bride on the front cover of *Matrimonial*, that is. The sight had hit her like a wake-up slap to the face. What was she thinking? She couldn't marry Matthias Barton. She couldn't marry a man for the same cold, cutthroat reasons her father picked a new business partner.

So she'd grabbed her keys and gathered her self-confidence and driven straight to where Matthias had mentioned he'd be staying for the next month, determined to get him out of her life.

Now she couldn't get him out of her mind.

Sighing, she turned away from the mirror and adjusted the spray in the shower. She'd found the master bedroom right off—my God, that luxurious bed had almost made her swoon!—but spun a quick about-face and entered a smaller guest bed and bath instead.

The hot water felt heavenly and some of her uneasiness went down the drain with it. All she had to do was walk back out there and tell that gorgeous hunk of a man that she wasn't marrying him. He'd probably be as relieved as she was. After that she'd drive home, face the certain-to-be-discordant music chez Conover and get on with the rest of her life.

The rest of her life that wouldn't include any more engagements to wrong men.

A few minutes later, wrapped in an oversized terry robe she'd found hanging on the bathroom door and carrying her damp clothes in hand, Lauren made her way to the staircase. Some framed photos lined the walls but she didn't give them but a cursory glance as she was more concerned with getting away from the house than anything. She could tell it was still raining and even from the second-floor landing the downstairs fire looked cozy and inviting, but she straightened her shoulders and mentally fused her vertebrae together.

Break it off, Lauren, she ordered herself as she descended the steps. *At once. Then get in your car and drive home.* Who cared about not waiting to dry the wet clothes? The robe covered her up just fine.

She could see Matthias standing by the fireplace now. He looked up…and somehow made her feel as if she wasn't wearing anything at all.

A flush heated all the skin under the suddenly scratchy terry cloth. Lauren's nipples hardened—though she wasn't the least bit cold, oh no sir—and she knew they were poking at the thick fabric. Would he notice? Could he tell?

Would he care?

Trying to pretend nothing was the least amiss, she made herself continue downward. But, man-oh-man, was he something to look at. He'd rolled up the sleeves of his dress shirt and unfastened a second button at the throat. The vee of undershirt she could see was blinding white and contrasted with the dark, past-five-o'clock stubble on his chin and around his mouth.

His mouth made her think of his kiss again. It was just a regular man's mouth, she supposed, but she liked the wideness of it and the deep etch of his upper lip. She really liked how it had felt on hers and, then, when his tongue had touched—

"Don't look at me like that," he suddenly said.

She was two steps from the bottom and the rasp in his voice made her grab for the railing. "I'm sorry," she said, unable to move, hardly able to speak. "What?"

"You look at me like that and I forget all about my intentions."

Her mouth went dry. "What intentions?" Maybe they were bad intentions…yet why did the idea of that sound so very good?

Matthias glanced over his shoulder. "My intention to feed you before anything else. Didn't I promise to rustle up dinner?"

Behind him she could see he'd set two places on the coffee table pulled up before a wide, soft-cushioned couch. Something was steaming—she could smell it, beef bourguignonne?—on two plates and ruby-colored liquid filled two wineglasses. Candles flickered in low votives.

Had she mentioned she was a sucker for candle-light?

She took another whiff of that delicious-smelling food. "Are you a good cook?"

He smiled and she liked that, too. His teeth were as white as his undershirt and they sent another wave of hot prickles across her flesh. "Maybe. Probably. But I've never tried."

She had to laugh at that. "Are you usually so confident? Even if you haven't attempted something you just expect you'll excel at it?"

"Of course. 'Assume success, deny failure.' My father taught us that."

"Yikes." And Lauren thought *her* cold-blooded *père* knew how to apply the screws. "That's a little harsh."

"You think so?" Matthias walked over to take her wet clothes in one hand and her free hand in the other.

He insinuated his long fingers between hers and the heat of his palm against hers shot toward her shoulder. "I think…I think…" Lauren couldn't remember what she was about to say. "Never mind."

He was smiling at her again, as if he understood her distraction. He led her toward the couch. "Let me put your clothes in the dryer, then we'll eat."

She stared after his retreating form for a moment, then started back to awareness. She was supposed to take the wet clothes home! Right after she told him the engagement was over! Right before walking out the door without dinner, without anything but her car keys and the comforting thought that she'd done the right thing.

But now he was coming toward her again, that small smile on his face and that appreciative light in his eyes. He brought that attraction between them back into the room, too—all that twitching, pulsing heat that drew her heart to her throat and her blood to several lower locations.

Tell him it's over! Her good sense shouted.

Tell him later, her sexuality purred, with a languid little stretch.

"Sit down," Matthias said, reaching out to touch her cheek.

Her knees gave way.

Merely postponing the inevitable. Lauren assured herself that she'd take care of what she came for and leave. Soon.

Except, an excellent dinner later, she was feeling a bit fuzzy from more merlot than she was used to. As well as a lot charmed by the man who had taken their dishes into the kitchen and was now sitting back on the cushions beside her, dangling the stem of his wine-glass between his fingers.

Over the meal he'd entertained her with stories that all revolved around his adventures in take-out dining. If she needed any further evidence that he was a business-obsessed workaholic like her father—and why else would Papa Conover have pushed so hard for her to marry Matthias?—now she had it. The man couldn't remember the last time he'd eaten food prepared in a home.

"Even this doesn't qualify, I'm afraid," he said, gesturing to where their plates had been. "The cartons were printed with the name of some gourmet catering place in town."

"Hunter's Landing, right?" Lauren asked. "Though it's not named after your friend from college? The one who built this house?"

Matthias shook his head. "No. Just a little joke on his part, I guess. He had a wild sense of humor."

The suddenly hoarse note in his voice made her throat tighten. He missed his friend, that was certain. Swallowing a sigh, she closed her eyes. This wasn't the way it was supposed to be. This wasn't the way *he* was supposed to be. She didn't want her parent-picked fiancé to be sexy or charming or vulnerable and, for God's sake, certainly not all three. It only made it that much harder to break it off with him.

She was always such a nitwit when it came to men. There was a reason she'd been engaged three times before now. There was a reason she'd picked the wrong men and then stuck with them until the humiliating end—until they walked out on her.

"So," Matthias said, breaking into her morose thoughts. "Enough about me. Tell me all about Lauren."

All about Lauren? Her eyes popped open and her spirits picked up. Was this the answer? If she told Mr. Assume-Success-Deny-Failure Barton all about Lauren, he might break it off between them himself! Because the truth was, when it came to romance, she was all about failure. And obviously more accustomed to getting dumped than the other way around.

Drawing her legs onto the couch, she turned on her side to face him.

Except his face was directed at her legs, bared by the edges of the terry robe that had opened with her movement. Heat rushing over her face, she yanked the fabric over her pale skin. She wasn't trying to come on to him. She was trying to get him to see that a marriage between the two of them would never work.

When she cleared her throat, he looked up, without a hint of shame on his face. "Great legs."

The compliment only served to discombobulate her further. The heat found its way to the back of her neck and she blurted out, "You know, you're fiancé number four."

He stared. "Number four?"

Ha. That had him. Now he'd turn off the charm and dam up that oozing sex appeal. She nodded. "I've been engaged before. Three other times."

He gave a small smile. "Optimistic little thing, aren't you?"

She frowned, bothered that he seemed more amused than appalled by her confession. Maybe he didn't believe her. Maybe he thought she was joking. Holding up her hand, she ticked them off. "Trevor, Joe and Jean-Paul."

"All right." He drained the remainder of his wine and set the glass on the table, as if ready for business. "Give me the down and dirty."

He still seemed amused. And charming. And sexy. Blast him.

Lauren took a breath. "I almost married Trevor when we were nineteen. It was going to be a sunset ceremony on the beach, followed by a honeymoon—one that I'd planned and paid for—that would hit all the best surfing spots in Costa Rica. On my wedding day, I was supposed to wear a white bandeau top, a grass skirt I found in a secondhand shop in Santa Cruz, and a crown of plumeria blossoms straight from Hawaii."

"Sounds fetching," he said, "though I don't see you as a surfer."

"That's probably the biggest reason Trevor ran off without me. He cashed in our first class tickets for coach ones and took his best surfing buddy to Central America instead. I haven't heard from him since."

Lauren experienced a little pang thinking of the bleached-blond she would always consider her first love. He'd driven her parents nuts, she recalled with a reminiscent smile. He'd been the perfect anti-Conover.

"Okay. That's number one. But why aren't you now Mrs. Joe…?"

"Rutkowski. His name is Joe Rutkowski."

Matthias bit his lip. "You're kidding."

"No. Joe Rutkowski was—well, *is*—my father's mechanic. If you find a good car-man, you don't break up with him—even if he breaks up with your daughter. That's what my father says, anyway."

"So what gave good ol' Joe second thoughts?"

"His pregnant other girlfriend."

"Oh."

"Little Jolene was born on my birthday, which also happened to be our proposed wedding date."

"Tell me you sent a baby gift. Little coveralls? A tiny timing light?"

Lauren narrowed her eyes at him. He didn't seem to be getting her point. "My heart was broken. My mother sent a certificate for a month of diaper service and signed my name." It still annoyed her that she'd lost the opportunity to watch her hoity-toity parents introduce the town's best Mercedes mechanic as their new son-in-law.

"But your broken heart recovered enough to find yourself in the arms of—what did you say his name was?—Jacques Cousteau?"

"Very funny. Jean-Paul Gagnon." Her father hated

Frenchmen. "I met him in Paris. We were going to get married on top of the Eiffel Tower. I had a tailored white linen suit with a long skirt that went to my ankles and was so tight that I couldn't run after the nasty little urchin who stole my purse on the way to the ceremony."

"I hope you're going to tell me that Jean-Paul took after the urchin himself."

"He did. But when he came back with my purse he told me that it had given him time to think about what he was doing. And marrying me was not what he wanted to do, after all." She gazed off into the distance, remembering her disappointment at not being able to shock her parents with the groom she brought home from Europe. "I really *liked* Jean-Paul."

"In the morning, I'll find some place that will feed you crepes."

In the morning? Lauren jerked her head toward him. "Have you been listening to a thing I said?"

"Of course I have." He moved closer and wrapped his hands around her wrists. "I just haven't figured out what the hell it has to do with you and me."

Lauren swallowed. Here was the opening she'd been waiting for. Now was the time to say, "There is no you and me, Matthias. There never really was."

Except the words wouldn't come out. They were stuck in her tight throat—and all it could handle was breathing, a task that seemed to be so much more complex when he was touching her.

"This is a lot harder than I thought," she whispered.

A ghost of a smile quirked one corner of his handsome mouth as he slid his fingers between hers. "You're telling me."

Despite her breathlessness, she found she could still laugh. "Are you being bad?"

"Not yet. But the night's still young."

Night? Good Lord, she'd completely lost track of time. It had been early evening just a minute ago. She checked her watch. "I've got to leave." Scooting back, she tried yanking her hands from his.

He merely held her tighter. "Not now, honey."

"But Matthias was…"

Something flickered in his eyes, but he didn't let go. "I may be an SOB, but I'm not completely black-hearted. It's too late, too dark, too stormy for me to let you leave tonight. It wouldn't be safe."

She looked out the windows and could tell he was right. The rain hadn't let up in the hours she'd been at the house and it was still coming down in torrents. Oh, great. She was stuck with the man she couldn't bring herself to break up with and her heart was thrumming so fast and he was so gorgeous she worried that if she didn't get away from him soon she'd… "I'm not so sure it's safe here, either."

"Will anyone be worrying about you? Do you need to make a call?"

Registering that he hadn't addressed the safety issue, she shook her head. "I had planned to stay with a friend in San Francisco for a few days on my way back. She said she'd expect me when she saw me."

"So here we are." He dropped her right hand so he could toy with one of her curls instead. "All alone on a dark and stormy night."

"So here we are," she echoed. "All alone." Oh, but her mother definitely could have called this one.

Coming up here was truly another of Lauren's Bad Ideas.

"How do you propose we entertain ourselves?" Matthias asked, twining a lock of her hair around his forefinger.

Lauren pretended not to notice. "Swap ghost stories? That sounds appropriate."

"But then we might be too scared to sleep."

Oh God. Her heart jumped and her gaze locked on his face. He was wearing that little smile again, as if he knew that mentioning the words *we* and *sleep* in the same sentence had her thinking of the two of them together, in a bed, doing everything *but* sleeping.

What the heck was going on? In the last few months, she'd chitchatted with Matthias at parties, danced with him a couple of times at charity events, pretended to be interested during family dinners while he talked shop with her father. Not once had she felt the slightest shiver of sexual attraction and now it was all she could do not to squirm in her seat.

Or squirm all over him.

"How come you weren't like this before?" she demanded.

His teeth flashed white. "I suppose I'll take that as a compliment."

"Seriously. Matthias—"

He put his hand over her mouth. "Shh. Don't talk."

She reached up to pull his fingers away. "If I don't talk I'm afraid I'll—"

And then he stopped that sentence, too, by swooping forward to kiss her for a second time. "Sorry," he said against her mouth. "I just can't help myself."

But *she* was helping him already by spearing her fingers through the crisp hair at the back of his head. He angled one way, she angled another and then they were *really* kissing, lips opening, tongues touching, tasting, their breaths and the sweet tang of merlot mingling.

Goose bumps rolled in a wave from the top of her scalp to the tickly skin behind her knees. She scooted closer to him, bumping the outside of his legs. Without breaking the connection of their mouths, he gathered her and the voluminous terry cloth onto his lap. In the move, the robe's hem rode up and she found herself settling onto him with nothing between her bare behind and his hard slacks-covered thighs.

Yanking her mouth from his, she glanced down, relieved to see that her front was covered decently enough and that the robe was draping her legs modestly, too. Still… "We shouldn't be doing this," she said, taking her hands from his hair.

"What?" His voice was hoarse.

Where to start? The engagement? The kiss? The lap? Or the bare skin which only felt barer because it was against the soft fabric that was clothing all those male muscles? "You know exactly what I'm talking about."

His eyelashes were spiky and dark, as masculine as the rest of him. "So you're holding out for the wedding night?"

The edge in his voice didn't surprise her. She felt edgy, too, torn between what her head was advising and what her body was demanding.

"We hardly know each other," she said. "So all this… this…"

"Hankering for hanky-panky?"

She narrowed her eyes at him. "…is a product of the rain, the wine, the—"

"The stone cold truth that we turn each other on hard and fast, Goldilocks, no explanations, no apologies. And to be honest, I'm as floored by it as you are."

"You are?" Not that she figured he considered her an ogre or anything, but the idea that this kind of "hankering for hanky-panky" wasn't standard for him, either, was a fascinating notion.

He laughed. "You look awfully pleased with yourself about it."

"Hey, in the past few years, I've been rejected on a regular basis, so forgive my dented ego for giving a little cheer." The merlot had seriously loosened her tongue.

"Fiancés one through four were idiots."

"*You're* number four," she reminded him.

"I'm trying to forget that." At the frown on her face, he shook his head and pinched her chin. "Goldilocks, I'm suggesting we try to forget everything but the fact that it's a dark and stormy night and we're alone together with our hankering. What do you say? Why not see where it takes us?"

She stared at him. "That's male reasoning."

He raised a dark eyebrow. "Cogent? To the point?"

"Shortsighted and all about sex."

"And your point is?"

Oh, he was making her laugh again. And *that* made her wiggle against his lap. And that made him groan and she was so…well, captivated by the powerful feeling the sound gave her that she leaned in to buss him on the mouth.

Which he turned into a real kiss.

Next thing she knew their tongues were twining and her hands were buried in his hair again. Heat was pouring off of him and his skin tasted a tiny bit salty as she kissed the corner of his mouth. "I want to bottle up this feeling," she told him, awed by its strength. Sexual chemistry, who knew? "We could market it and make a kabillion dollars."

"A kabillion is a lot," he murmured, then turned his attention to her left ear.

Goose bumps sprinted across every inch of her skin as his tongue feathered over the rim to tickle the lobe. "A kabillion-ten," she corrected herself. "In the first year."

He traveled back to her mouth, then took his time there, leisurely playing with all the surfaces. Her breath backed up in her lungs when he sucked her bottom lip into his mouth. Her fingers tightened on his scalp when he slid the tip of his tongue along the damp skin inside her upper lip. She moaned when he thrust inside her mouth, filling her with his purpose and male demand.

And all the while she was excruciatingly aware of her nakedness under the robe. Of her bareness resting against his pant legs. The soft wool scratched at her skin now, sensitized as it was by the kisses that never let up and the hands that never wandered beyond her hair and her face.

She was fast losing all the reasons why she should be happy about that. In the face of this "hankering" as he called it, she'd been unable to stand up against the kissing. It wasn't such a bad thing, though, was it? For goodness sake, she *was* engaged to the man.

Still.

A little voice somewhere in the dim recesses of her mind reminded her she was here to put an end to that engagement, but she shushed the crabby killjoy. Because this man could *kiss*, and there was no reason to deny herself the pleasure.

Except that kissing was quickly becoming not quite enough.

To ease the growing ache, she squeezed her thighs together and wiggled her naked behind. Matthias tore his lips from hers to gaze at her with serious eyes. "You're making me crazy." His mouth was wet.

She dried it with the edge of her thumb. "What'd you say?" She stroked her thumb the other way and he caught it between his teeth. Nipped.

Lauren shivered once and then again when his tongue swiped over her fingertip. The inside of his mouth was hot and wet and she leaned forward to taste it again.

He caught her shoulders, keeping her a breath away. "Lauren, maybe you were right…"

"Just one more." She pushed at his hands and, as they fell, they took the robe with them. It dropped to her waist.

Leaving her naked from her belly button up.

And frozen between caution and desire.

His gaze stayed on her face, but when she made no move to cover herself, he let it wander southward. Slowly.

Like a caress, she felt it move across her features, from her nose, to her mouth, over her chin and then down the column of her neck.

It traced the edges of her collarbone and her breath caught, held, as he finally stared at her breasts. Under the weight of his gaze, her nipples went from tight to tighter. She glanced down, noticing how hard and darker they looked against the pale skin of her swollen breasts.

Without thinking, she moved her arms up to cover herself.

"Don't." He caught her wrists. "Don't keep them from me."

Hot chills tumbled down her naked spine. She didn't want to keep them from him. She didn't want to keep any part of herself from him.

In a blur of movement, he stood, lifting her in his arms. "Wh—?" she began.

"Shh," he said. "Don't talk." He strode for the staircase, rushing up the steps as if she weighed nothing.

She felt weightless, too, as if she were floating on a cloud of desire. And a cloud of impossible dreams. Good God, could her parents have been right? Had they picked the right man for her after all?

He didn't hesitate at the top of the stairs, but headed straight for the master bedroom. At the foot of the enormous sleigh bed, he hesitated.

Lauren rested her head against his chest, his heart beating hard and fast in her ear. There was nothing she wanted more than to get naked, completely naked, with him. She smiled up at his face, seductively, she thought. "Matthias? Aren't you going to make love to me?"

Three

Lauren stirred, stretched, came awake to the knowledge that she was in a strange bed in a strange room, wearing a near-stranger's T-shirt and nothing else. A trio of emotions washed through her. Relief. Embarrassment. Annoyance that her parent-picked fiancé proved to be more cautious and in control of his libido than she was of hers.

Last night, when she'd said, "Matthias? Aren't you going to make love to me?" he'd gone still and silent. Further prodding, "Matthias? Matthias?" had caused him to close his eyes as if in pain. Then he'd taken a long deep breath and replied, "No."

In less than forty-five seconds he'd left her in the guest bedroom with one of his shirts and a kiss on the nose.

You had to hate that kind of self-control in a man.

But now it was morning and from the quiet sound of it, the rain had stopped, so she was free to take herself and her humiliation out of his house. She'd give herself a pass on breaking off the engagement in person. When she got a safe one-hundred miles or so away, she'd give him a call. Better yet, she'd send an e-mail from an anonymous account. Or perhaps a note by slow-flying carrier pigeon.

She wasn't going to face him again, even if it meant driving home in a knee-length T-shirt and nothing else.

A woman who wasn't yet thirty and yet who'd been rejected at both the altar and in the bedroom didn't need to eat any more humble pie, thank you very much.

However, she wasn't destined for near-naked driving that day. When she inched open the bedroom door, she found a neat pile of her dried clothing. Once she'd pulled it on, she crossed to the door again, listened to the quiet for a moment, then tiptoed along the hall and down the stairs on the first leg of her furtive escape.

Only to find her host was watching her take those ex-aggerated silent footsteps over the rim of a coffee cup.

"Oh, uh, hi." She tried tacking on a casual expression to convince him that strutting like a soundless rooster was one of her normal morning activities. "I didn't, um, see you there."

Seeing him was the problem! Seeing him reminded her of what he'd looked like last night, smiling at her, touching her hair, her face, coming close-up for kisses that were burned into her mind. Crossing her arms over her chest, she tried banishing the memories of his dark gaze on her naked breasts.

How *much* she'd wanted him to touch her.

In an abrupt move, he half turned away, the liquid in his cup sloshing dangerously close to the edge. "Are you ready for that breakfast I promised?"

"Breakfast?" She sounded stupid, but she felt stupid that even *sans* merlot, cozy firelight and distant drumming of the rain, her attraction to him was alive and quite, quite well.

Her attraction to the man who'd been able to deny everything she'd offered him last night.

"I said I'd feed you." He turned back. "And if I don't get some decent caffeine I might start gnawing on table legs. I freely admit to being a coffee snob and this stuff isn't up to my usual standards. This stuff is instant. There isn't anything else in the house."

"Oh. Well. Then." She would have liked nothing better than to grab her keys and get out of there, but she was suddenly rediscovering that spine of hers. And her pride. Instead of running off like a cowardly ninny, she'd spend another hour with him.

Then she'd hide off someplace where she could rent a pigeon.

An hour without making a further fool of herself. That shouldn't be so hard, should it?

She chalked up the silence of the car ride into the tiny town of Hunter's Landing to his need for quality caffeine. For herself, she managed to clamp down on her usual nervous babble by digging her fingernails into her palms whenever she felt compelled to volley a conversational gambit.

She was afraid a neutral comment intended to sound like "Beautiful morning, isn't it?" might come out as a plaintive "Why didn't you go to bed with me last night?"

So she created some half-moon marks in her hands and applied herself to observing the view outside his SUV's windows. It *was* a beautiful morning. The road was narrow and windy, taking them through heavy woods with pine boughs that still held raindrops winking like crystals in the sunlight. Every once in a while she'd catch a glimpse of the lake, its deep blue a match of the spring sky overhead.

As they neared the town, there was a slow-moving parade of "traffic"—actually a short line of cars in both directions that were pulling into or out of parking lots of small stores and cafés. Matthias glanced over at her. "Have you been to the lake before?"

She nodded. "But only during ski season."

"You downhill? Cross-country? Snowboard?"

"Truth? I'm best at hot chocolate and stoking the fire."

He grinned. "A woman after my own heart."

Ha. After last night, they both knew that wasn't true. "What, you don't like snow activities that much either?"

"No, I like all sorts of snow activities. But when I'm done playing, I like a warm beverage, a warm fire and a warm woman waiting."

She curled her lip at him. "That's an incredibly sexist thing to say."

He steered the car into a parking space outside a restaurant called Clearwater's. "Hey, I didn't say I expected it to be that way, only that I liked it. Since you do, too, I don't see the problem."

What did he mean by that? Did he mean he didn't see the problem that she had with his comment or that, given their natural proclivities, he didn't think they'd have a problem with their marriage during ski season?

Except they weren't getting married. And she wasn't going to bother making that point in case he really was only referring to the comment and he'd think her assumption about thinking he was referring to their marriage incredibly presumptuous. Oh, God. Now she was babbling to herself.

Get out of the car, Lauren. Get out. Eat breakfast and don't make a fool of yourself for a single, simple hour.

They were shown to a table by the window, over-looking a spectacular view of the lake. Boats of all shapes and sizes were already on the water and Lauren shivered, thinking how chilly it must be out in the wind. Matthias had given her a sweater of his before they left the house and she was grateful for the soft warmth.

And the delicious smell of him that clung to it.

She shivered again.

Matthias looked over his open menu. "You all right?"

"Sure." She looked down at the offerings to avoid gazing at his face. Unlike last night, he was close-shaven now, and she itched to run her fingers along the smooth line of his jaw. *Don't do something dumb, Lauren.*

"Sorry about this, but I don't see crepes."

She glanced up. "Crepes?"

"Remember? I was going to get them for you as a way of making up for Gaston's absence in your life."

"*Gagnon*. Jean-Paul Gagnon. Gaston is from Disney's *Beauty and the Beast*. You know, the ego-inflated villain."

"See? I was right after all."

She found herself smiling at him.

He reached out and brushed her bottom lip. "I like that. You've been very serious this morning."

Her gaze dropped back to her menu while her lip throbbed in reaction to his light touch. "I need my caffeine, too."

"Amazing how compatible we are," he murmured.

She pretended not to hear him. Compatibility made her think of marriage again and made her wonder if *he* was thinking of marriage, and also made her wonder if he was really seriously considering putting a wedding band on her finger or if was he going to dump her like all her other fiancés had.

No, wait. See how confused he made her? She was going to be dumping *him*.

The waitress came by, served up the gourmet caffeine, then took their order. They sipped coffee until the food arrived—the whole nine yards for him, oatmeal and fruit for her—and she had a mouthful of the brown-sugary stuff when he spoke again.

"You know, I just realized I'm not completely clear on why you came to the house last night."

To give herself thinking time, she pointed to her full mouth and did the whole pantomime that translated to "just a second, let me chew and swallow." Once the spoonful was on its way to her stomach, however, the best she could come up with was misdirection.

"Well, you know, I'm not completely clear on why

you're at that beautiful house in the first place." She held her breath, hoping he'd fall for her ruse.

"I didn't mention it?"

"Nope. Not exactly why you're living there. My father was the one who gave me the address. I only know that it has something to do with your college friend Hunter."

He cleared his throat. "Hunter Palmer."

"I think my family knows some Palmers. Palm Springs? Bel-Air?"

Luke nodded. "That's his family. Pharmaceuticals and personal-care products. We met in college. There was a group of us, we called ourselves the Seven Samurai."

Lauren smiled. "And you males think *The Sisterhood of the Traveling Pants* sounds silly."

He sipped at his coffee. "Ours was a special friendship, I'll give you that."

"Tell me about them."

"We were all privileged sons of prestigious families. But what brought us together was that we weren't content to merely suck from straws stuck in family trust funds. We wanted to make our own ways, our own marks. And we did. We have."

The conviction in his voice made him only more interesting. "How does that relate to a Lake Tahoe log house?"

The quick flash of a grin. "Oh, well, that's a bit less noble. I think it was the beer talking. No, it was definitely the beer talking."

She laughed. "Thank you for showing the statues' feet of clay."

"I won't mention the aching heads the next morning."

"Oh, come on. Tell."

He pulled his coffee cup closer and stared into the black liquid as if it was a screen on the past. A small smile quirked the edges of his lips. "After a little too much partying one night, we made a pact that in ten years, we'd build a house on Lake Tahoe. Then we'd live there in successive months, meeting after the last one to celebrate all that we were certain we would have accomplished."

The smile deepened and he looked up to meet her gaze. "I'll say it for you. Arrogant brats."

She put her elbow on the table and rested her chin on her hand. "I don't know. You said that you arrogant brats had done what you set out to do."

"Guess so." He shrugged. "Besides me, there's Nathan Barrister, who continues making money hand-over-fist for his family's hotel chain; Ryan Matheson, who has his own pockets full of cable companies; Devlin Campbell, über-banker; and Jack Howington, our adventurer."

"That's only five," she pointed out.

"You know that Hunter died. Right before graduation." His gaze returned to his coffee. "I still miss him."

Lauren's heart squeezed, but she could still count. "That makes six."

His coffee appeared to fascinate him. "And then there's my brother."

She'd wondered if he'd be able to bring himself to mention his twin. Though she was aware of their estrangement, she didn't know the particulars. It seemed

a shame—but then she'd never met Luke Barton.
Maybe he really was enemy number one.

"Let's not talk about him," Matthias said.

The sudden strain in his voice and the tension in his
expression made Lauren want to, though.

"Let's talk about you instead," he continued.

Lauren started. Uh-oh. Not her. Talk about her could
lead to trouble. The kind where she ended up humili-
ated again.

"I already know about the fiancés in your past. But
I don't know much about your work—"

"You know I'm a freelance translator." Okay. Work
was a safe topic. She could talk about work. "It pays
well, even though my father was sure my dual degrees
in French and Spanish would never amount to
anything."

"That's why you were in Paris?"

She nodded. "A long-term project. Unfortunately, I
had to give up my apartment before I left the States, so
now I'm back with Mom and Dad until—"

"The convenient merger of the Bartons and the
Conovers," he inserted, a new, hard edge to his voice.

A shiver rippled down Lauren's back, not a sexy
shiver, but a what's-going-on-here warning. Her expression must have betrayed her dismay, because he
reached over for her hand.

"Sorry," he said, squeezing her fingers. "Don't mind
me."

The fact that the marriage would be good for both
family businesses had been hammered home to her by
her father. Wrapped up in the cotton wool of what she
had to acknowledge now was likely a depression, she'd

barely felt a prick of worry over it. And she'd assumed Matthias was happy about that part of the deal. He didn't look happy now.

"Look…" she started.

"Shh." He lifted her hand and kissed her knuckles.

There was that other shiver. The one she was now familiar with when she was around him. It tickled up her arm and trailed down her back.

Without breaking her gaze, he ran his thumb across her knuckles. "I'm a bastard."

"I thought something similar myself last night," Lauren heard herself say—then wished it back with all her might. Dang it. Dang it! *Humiliation, here I come.*

Matthias's hand tightened on hers. "I—"

"Don't bother coming up with an excuse," she said hastily. "You were right. That was smart. We barely know each other and the bedroom isn't the best way to rectify that. Cooler heads prevailed. Give the man first prize."

"Lauren…"

She knew her face must be red because she felt heat from her neck on up. And she was babbling like she always did when she was uncomfortable, but it was too late to alter a lifetime's bad habit now. "I should thank you. I do. Thank you. Thank you very much. I appreciate your restraint and your…uh…uh…disinterest."

"Disinterest?" He was staring at her as if she'd grown another head. She wanted to take the single one she did have and bang it against the tabletop.

"Did you say *disinterest*?"

She tried to pull her hand from his. "Maybe. No. Yes. Whatever you think you heard I probably said."

"Hell!" He threw his napkin onto the table. "That's

it. We're done." He stood up, threw some bills on the table, then pulled her from her chair. Her napkin fell to the floor but he didn't give her time to pick it up. Instead, he hustled her out of the restaurant then started walking, dragging her along beside him.

There was a pretty footpath along the lake, but she didn't get much chance to appreciate the view because his long strides made her nearly run to keep up. When they reached a small covered lookout, he yanked her inside and then dropped onto the wooden bench. She was tugged down beside him.

"For the record, I was *not* disinterested last night," he said. "How could you even think that?"

"Uh, guest room? Long T-shirt? The way you practically ran away?"

"I was trying to be a good guy, you know that."

"Bet that's what my three previous fiancés told themselves, too."

He groaned. "Lauren."

Maybe she was being a tad unreasonable. Remember, she'd been grateful this morning that he'd showed restraint last night.

Oh, who was she kidding? She'd been mostly irritated that he'd been all dazzle but no follow-through. And she'd been hurt. And in serious doubt about her particular powers to ever really capture and keep the interest of a man.

"I've been going through a bad stretch, okay?" she said. "And there I was, practically begging, and you backed away. It's…"

Mortifying. And, oh, now even more so, as she felt the sting of tears at the corners of her eyes. She jerked her face away from his and toward the lake. "My, this wind is brisk, isn't it?"

He groaned again. "Lauren. Lauren, please." His fingers grasped her chin and he brought her face back to his. "Damn it. Last night, this morning, right now, I've been frustrated in four thousand different ways. My good intentions are running on empty, Goldilocks, and—oh, forget it."

Then he kissed her again.

Finally.

It tasted wonderful…and perhaps a touch angry.

"It's just so good," she whispered against his mouth.

He buried one hand in her hair as he deepened the kiss. The other hand slipped under his own oversized sweater to mold her breast. Her nipple contracted to a hard, desperate point. His thumb grazed over it.

As payback, Lauren ran her hand up his lean thigh to cup the hard bulge in his jeans. He jerked against her palm and his thumb moved over her nipple again. Harder.

She moaned. *It's just so good.*

So good that bells were ringing.

Matthias yanked his mouth from hers. "Hell." His hand left her, too, as he stood and dug in his front pocket.

The bells were still ringing. No, the *cell phone* was still ringing. Matthias's BlackBerry. He looked at the screen, muttered another curse, then pointed a finger at her. "Stay there," he barked, then ducked out of the little shelter.

Boneless, she fell back against the bench's seat. Now that she'd come clean about her feelings, she wasn't going anywhere. It hadn't been so humiliating after all. It had felt a lot more like heaven.

The call was from Luke's Eagle Wireless office. He ran his hand through his hair, trying to cool himself down before answering. Lauren had walked straight out of his fantasies to wreak havoc on his self-control and it didn't help that the sexual attraction ran so fast and hot both ways. Last night he'd come too close to letting sex take over his common sense.

He needed to get her out of the log house and away from him. She needed to go back to where she belonged. Back to her life.

Back to his brother.

That last thought took a vicious bite of him and he took it out on his assistant as he answered the call. "What do you want?"

"Good morning to you, too, Mary Sunshine."

He ignored her sarcastic rejoinder, then forgot it completely when she told him the reason she'd rung. She wanted to patch a call through from his brother.

"You know I don't talk to him." They hadn't spoken in seven years. Seven, like the Seven Samurai. Something about that stabbed like an ice pick to the chest, but he rubbed the useless feeling away. "Tell him to go to hell."

"He thought you'd say that. He told me to inform you he's in Germany, so you know he's already been there."

Luke almost laughed. Matt hated to travel overseas. Foreign flights, foreign food, foreign beds, they all put his brother off eating and sleeping. So why was his twin in Europe? Luke's mind raced through the possibilities, then locked on one that made the hair on the back of his neck rise. *Germany*. Anger burned like fire up his spine.

"Patch him through, Elaine."

And then there was Matt's voice. Tired, a little hoarse, but so damn familiar. "Yo, brother."

So damn familiar and so damn traitorous.

"Why are you in Germany?" Luke demanded.

"Is that any way to talk to the man who is calling to see how things are going at Hunter's house? I know you did this as a favor and—"

"I didn't do this as a favor to *you,* you bastard, and you know it. I agreed so that your 'last-minute business trip' wouldn't screw up Hunter's last wishes and now it looks as if you're screwing me over."

"I don't know what you're talking about."

"You're in Stuttgart, aren't you?" Stuttgart, the home base of a supplier Luke had been wooing for the last eight months. The deal he'd been nurturing would double his domestic profits. Triple the money he could make in China. He'd heard rumors that Conover Industries had been sniffing around, but Ralph Conover couldn't put together the kind of package that Luke could. Neither could Matt—not unless he got into bed with Conover.

Or Conover's daughter.

Damn them. Damn all of them.

"You're not going to cheat me this time, Matt," he ground out.

"I didn't cheat you *any* time, lunkhead."

Lunkhead. It was the name Matt had coined for him when they were kids. When they'd hated each other as much as they hated each other now. Only in college, those brief years when they'd really felt like brothers, had the nickname been said with affection.

"I don't have anything more to say to you." He flipped off the phone.

Shoving it in his pocket, he stared out at the lake, trying to get himself under control. That thieving bastard had tricked Luke into taking his place at Hunter's house so that he could head off to Germany undeterred and take over the deal that belonged to Eagle Wireless. Maybe Ernst would be loyal to what he'd already started with Luke. Maybe not.

Hell, probably not.

Loyalty wasn't something Luke had much faith in.

What he wouldn't give to screw over his brother as Matt had screwed over him! Just once, just once, Luke would like to take something that was his brother's. Then Matt would see what it was like to feel that sharp stab in the back from the one person who was supposed to be *watching* his back.

Luke turned to head back to his car and his gaze caught on the wooden lookout. Lauren. Hell, he'd nearly forgotten her.

Even as angry as he was, a little grin broke over his face. If he'd left her there she would have his liver for dinner. Sweet Lauren, who had thought he'd left her alone last night because he was disinterested! Sexy Lauren, who could be the model for the co-star in every hot dream he'd ever had.

He jogged over to the shelter and grabbed her hand to pull her up. "Let's go."

"Where?" She smiled.

Lauren smiled. Lauren who was engaged to his brother. Lauren who was Ralph Conover's daughter.

An idea, an oh-so-fitting idea, started creeping from a dark corner of his mind. And Luke let it. Then he pulled her against him and dropped a kiss on her bottom lip.

She looked up at him. Sweet. Sexy. Trusting.

"We never cleared up why you showed up at the house last night," Luke said.

Her eyes rounded. Her tongue darted out to wet her lower lip.

"No," she answered slowly.

Thinking back to all the things she'd said and the others she'd hinted at, Luke thought maybe she'd come to break the engagement. And if she *had* decided to give Matt the old heave-ho, then Luke would let her go. But after this month was up, if he still couldn't get her out of his head, he'd contact her and see if she felt the same way. He'd make it clear that Luke Barton was only after fun and games, but if she wanted to play, he was ready for a round or two.

However, if she was actually serious about this business-deal merger-marriage with Matt…

He had to find out for sure.

"So why'd you come, Lauren?"

"Ummm…"

He could hear the wheels turning in her head. "It's a simple question, Goldilocks." His fingers brushed back the hair from her forehead and a flush rose on her cheeks.

"I came to…umm…"

Her hair blew across her eyes and he caught it, then tucked it behind her ear. She shivered at his touch.

"Goldilocks?"

"I came to get to know you better," she blurted out. Her flush deepened. "We *are* barely acquainted and we *are* engaged, after all, and engaged people should know each other, don't you think? Because really…"

She continued chattering away, but he had stopped listening. He already had his answer. She hadn't come here to break it off with Matt.

Meaning Luke had in his hands right now, this minute, something that cheating, thieving Matt Barton wanted.

Oh, it was going to be sweet, sweet revenge when Matt discovered Luke had set out to seduce his brother's bride.

Luke wasn't going to feel bad about it.

Certainly not on Matt's behalf.

And not on Lauren's, either.

Because, after all, it was up to her whether or not he succeeded.

Four

Matthias pulled Lauren in the direction of the restaurant. "Let's go back to the house," he said.

She swallowed and tried hanging back. "Um. Uh. Right now?"

"You said you wanted to get to know me better."

Lauren's pulse quickened. Yes, yes, she'd said that, but there was a new, predatory gleam in her fiancé's eyes and maybe it was time to take a few deep breaths.

Back at the house there would be that decadent, quilt-covered bed, but would there be air?

"I was thinking it might be fun to explore the town," she said, slipping out of Matthias's hold. "You know. Look around." Which would give her time to consider her options and decide whether she should stay or whether she should go.

Matthias slid his hands in his pockets. "I don't know what there is to see," he said, sounding impatient.

"That's the whole point," Lauren replied. "Finding out what there is to see."

He paused a moment, then gave a little shrug followed by a small smile. She got the feeling he'd diagnosed her stall tactic and was indulging it…for the moment.

"Fine," he said, taking off at a pace so fast that his long legs ate up the path that would take them back toward the restaurant and, from there, to the rest of the little town of Hunter's Landing.

Lauren had to jog to catch up with him and her pace was still hurried as they traversed the streets of the small town, passing small shops, businesses and cafés. At the end of what Lauren supposed the residents called "downtown" sat the post office and Matthias paused beside the American flag that was flapping in the brisk breeze.

The wind fluttered his dark hair and tousled it over his forehead. The cool air or the sun or both had washed a tinge of ruddy color over the rise of his cheekbones and reddened his lips. Lauren stared at them, remembering the kisses from last night, how the burr of his evening beard had burned the tender edges of her mouth, rendering each caress hotter than the one before. She pressed the back of her hand over her own lips and shivered at the memory.

His eyes narrowed. "You're cold," he said. "And you've seen the whole of Hunter's Landing. Ready to go back now?"

Ready to go back? She shook her head. Not when

just the thought of kissing him continued to be so distracting. She needed more time.

"We've done the town," Matthias said, frowning. "What more do you want?"

That was easy. She wanted an un-befuddled head, one that wasn't affected by these inexplicable hormone rushes. She cleared her throat. "We haven't done the town, we rushed through it. Haven't you heard of strolling? Of enjoying the fresh air and the beautiful day?"

"To what end?"

She blinked. To what end? Must there always be an end? Obviously, the man needed to learn to relax. But he was already jiggling the change in his pocket, ready for action, so she gazed around her and hit upon inspiration.

"There. Coffee," she said, pointing across and down the street. A small shop called Java & More. "Didn't you say the house needs a fancier blend? I'll bet we can get some freshly ground at that store."

It worked. Sort of. Matthias set off in the direction she'd indicated, but first he slid his arm around her shoulders. And then, when she shivered in reaction, he drew her close against the side of his body.

"I'll keep you warm," he said, hugging her close as they crossed the street.

Too warm. Oh, much too warm.

Her hip bumped against him with each step. His fingers were five hot brands on the curve of her shoulder. He was near enough that she could feel the heat of his breath against her temple and the sensation made her skin jitter in reaction. His hand slid to the nape of her neck and gave a little squeeze. She glanced up.

Their eyes met and there it was again, an almost audible sexual snap, and it had her stumbling on the sidewalk. Matthias's hand tightened once more to keep her upright and she found herself leaning against him, her heart fluttering like that flag across the street, her nipples tightening as if they could feel the cold instead of all this delicious heat. With his free hand, he tilted her chin higher.

Tilting her mouth to his, he brushed his thumb across her bottom lip.

Heat tumbled from that point, rushing like a fall of water over her breasts and toward her womb. Lauren clutched his hard side as support for her rubbery knees.

His thumb feathered over her lip a second time. "Come back to the house," he whispered.

She watched his mouth descend.

"Come back to the house right now." He murmured it against her lips.

His kiss tasted like coffee and maple syrup and seduction.

It was a gentle press of mouth-to-mouth and she softened instantly, without thinking anything beyond how right it felt to be kissing this man. He angled his head to take it deeper and she opened her lips for him, but he did nothing more than breathe inside her mouth.

She wanted the thrust of his tongue!

He wasn't giving it up.

He was waiting for her.

Lauren felt heat again, flushing over all her skin. Matthias was waiting for *her* to make the next move. Waiting for her to make a decision. But before she could, a car honked.

The sudden noise caused her to jerk back. Matthias didn't move, though, instead remaining close and watching her with that same hungry light in his eyes she'd noticed after he'd returned from his phone call. It scared her.

Liar, it called to her.

Here was a man, not a boy-surfer, not a two-timing mechanic, not an intellectual yet indecisive cosmopolitan. Here was a one-hundred-percent red-blooded, single-minded American male animal who knew exactly what he wanted.

Her.

And she *did* want to get to know him better. She wanted to get to know *everything* about him. Her blood felt thick in her veins, and her heart beat harder inside her chest to move it through her body.

"Matthias." Her voice came out so hoarse that she had to clear her throat and start again. "Matthias. I'm ready to go back to the house."

He smiled. The fingers holding her chin slid down to caress the soft skin beneath and then to stroke along her neck. His thumb found the notch of her collarbone and rested there a moment. "A kabillion one hundred," he said.

The value of their bottled sexual chemistry had just gone up.

Taking her hand in his, Matthias turned them both back in the direction of the car and took off again at his brisk pace.

"We can still make a quick stop for the coffee," she said as they passed the shop.

He paused, and just then another couple exited the

door of Java & More. They weren't looking at them, they weren't looking at anything but each other, yet something about the two galvanized Matthias. Murmuring an indecipherable phrase beneath his breath, he quickly pushed her forward and then through the door of the neighboring business.

Lauren looked around the dim confines and found herself in teen paradise—a place stuffed with video-game and pinball machines, Skee-Ball ramps, an air-hockey table and a counter with a bored guy presumably able to provide change if only he'd look up from his magazine. Matthias shot a look out the streaky front window and guided Lauren farther inside.

"No pool table?" he murmured. "Hell, fine then." His fingers on the small of her back proceeded her toward an air-hockey table. He fished in his pocket for those coins that had been jangling earlier.

"You play?" he said, glancing out the front window once more. "Let's play. First to seven points wins."

Since her little sister Kaitlyn had walked all over her at a similar table not long before, Lauren released a sigh, but didn't try to talk him out of it. She might be an altar reject, but she wasn't completely clueless. For some reason Matthias wanted to avoid that other couple. They'd looked harmless enough to her—a man about Matthias's age and a woman about her own, in love, but she didn't have more time to ponder the situation because already Matthias was flinging that air-hockey puck in her direction.

Her hand grabbed her mallet to make an instinctive defensive move.

And her instincts—as was obvious by the three

previous broken engagements—weren't worth an anthill of beans. She lost the first game seven-zip. And the game after that. And the game after that.

A crowd of teens gathered around the table. She couldn't understand exactly why until Matthias barked something to one of them and she realized they were checking out her backside. Apparently the place—not to mention the young men—was sorely lacking from a dearth of the female gender. It did smell like a gym after an afternoon of six-man dodgeball. On a rainy day.

Following her three losses she conceded defeat, hoping they could go on their way, but when she stepped back from the table, a stringy-bodied, stringy-haired teenager stepped up in her place and slammed his quarters on the edge of the table. Lauren gathered it was some sort of challenge and, like a scene out of an old Western, Matthias's eyes took on a new gleam and he slammed his quarters down in return.

The competition was on.

And on.

Without a word being spoken about it, as Matthias defeated each challenger, another came to stand in his place. He met each one with the same ruthless intensity as the contender before: his sleeves pushed up to his elbows, his face a mask of concentration, his stance wide and aggressive. At first Lauren was amused and then a bit admiring—the muscles of his forearm flexed in a purely masculine manner—and then…and then she was alarmed by the obvious ferocity of his desire to win.

After a while it was clear he wasn't aware that she was there or aware of where he was or aware of anything but slamming that puck into the goal, over and over and over.

"Matthias…" she ventured.

He didn't flick her a glance as another player stepped in to replace the one he'd defeated.

"Matthias."

No response.

"Matthias!"

He started, then his head swiveled toward her. She saw him blink as if coming out of a fog.

"Assume success, deny failure?" she asked.

He frowned. "What?"

"Is that what this is all about? Victory at all costs, no matter what?" She tried to make light of it, but the way he looked when he played wasn't funny. The way he was looking at her now wasn't funny either.

"What's wrong with wanting to win?" His voice was puzzled. "What's wrong with hating to fail?"

Nothing, unless that was *all* you'd been taught. If you'd never learned that it was okay to fall down sometimes and how to pick yourself up if you did. Lauren thought of her three unsuccessful attempts at marriage.

Losing was something she wished she didn't know so much about.

She cleared her throat and changed the subject. "I thought we were going back to the house."

"There's a competitor…" His voice trailed off as he looked across the table at the scruffy boy who was no more than four feet tall. "It's a kid."

"Matthias, they've all been kids."

He looked around at the faces ringing the table. Then with a half-smile that was more a grimace, he stepped back from the table. "Um, all done for today. Thanks for the games."

He took Lauren's arm and started for the front door. "Okay. I admit it. I got a bit carried away."

Outside the place—named The Game Palace, she now saw—they both paused, adjusting to the bright sunshine. "I thought you'd forgotten all about me," Lauren said, her tone light. "I guess I'll need to take air-hockey lessons to keep some of your attention."

She was teasing, of course, but when he turned to face her, she could see that he was serious again. "Sweetheart, after last night, I know you don't need lessons in the kind of thing that will keep *all* of my attention."

The flush moved up her body this time, a warm wash that surely covered her face to the roots of her hair. "Matthias…"

"Lauren…" His voice echoed hers as he drew a fingertip from her earlobe to the corner of her mouth. "Let's go back now. Let's take the time to learn everything we can about each other."

"Does that mean you're going to tell me all your secrets?"

His finger paused in its wandering. "That might take a while."

She had a while. She had a lifetime, if he was the right man. And suddenly she realized that she was stronger than she'd first thought. Yes, he was sexy, charming and vulnerable in a way that tugged at her from many different directions, but she wasn't going to let those qualities tumble her immediately into his bed.

"Let's go back to the house," she said. "But once we're there, we need to discuss some rules."

"I don't like rules," Matthias cautioned, slanting her a glance from his corner of the living-room couch.

Lauren grimaced. After their return from Hunter's Landing, she'd managed to keep her fiancé distracted for a while by exploring the grounds and then the interior of the luxurious log-and-stone house. It had been built under the auspices of the Hunter Palmer Foundation and, once all of the Seven Samurai had completed their month-long stays, the place would be turned into an R&R retreat for recovering cancer patients—something Hunter himself had understood the need for, presumably, as he'd died of melanoma.

While a couple of the bedroom suites were decorated, as well as most of the living spaces, it was obvious that there was some decorating yet to be done. Still, the whole setup was incredible and it didn't surprise her that her business-oriented fiancé had been drawn to the state-of-the-art office that occupied the loft on the third floor. When she'd made noises about wanting to relax and read for a bit, he'd immediately headed up the stairs with his laptop and didn't come down until the hands of the grandfather clock in the foyer announced it was five o'clock.

After a brief stop in the kitchen, he'd found her in the great room. He'd handed over one of the glasses of wine he was carrying before taking his seat, from which he made that *un*surprising announcement: *I don't like rules.*

Lauren inspected herself for any imaginary lint as

she debated how to answer. While he was mired in work, she'd finally recollected and then retrieved from her car the small weekender bag she'd packed in anticipation of visiting her former college roommate in San Francisco. Now she wore a fresh pair of jeans and a cream-colored cashmere sweater she'd bought in Paris.

"My little sister Kaitlyn has rules that govern just about everything."

"You have a sister?"

Lauren looked up at him in surprise. "You've met her a couple of times, remember? Thirteen? Braces?"

"Of course." Matthias's gaze shifted from her face to the window. "I wasn't thinking..."

Lauren took a breath. "That's where I want to do things differently, Matthias. I want to think before I leap."

"You're doubting that the fourth time's a charm?"

Her face heated at his reference to her three botched engagements. "I'm talking about this...this attraction between us. I'm doubting whether it's smart to act on it and tumble into a sexual relationship so quickly. Aren't you willing to applaud my caution? After all, it's your marriage, too."

Matthias's gaze shifted away again. "Tell me about Kaitlyn and her rules."

Lauren smiled. "Besides the old standbys about avoiding sidewalk cracks and lines, these days she approaches her mirror backward, only whirling around when she's ready to see herself. According to Kaitlyn, true beauty only comes upon you by surprise, so..." Her hands rose.

"If she looks anything like her sister, the question of beauty isn't any question at all."

"Thank you." The compliment pleased her more than she wanted it to. "You've seen Kaitlyn for yourself. No matter how pretty we tell her she is, she's at that hyper-self-critical age. You remember thirteen, right?"

"Yeah." He took a swallow from his glass. "Come to think of it, when my brother and I hit thirteen our father laid a whole list of rules on us."

This was the kind of thing she wanted to know! That his kiss was divine, that he smelled like heaven, that his hands on her was something she desired more with each passing minute—that kind of knowledge was pleasing, but it certainly didn't promise a happy marriage.

She circled her forefinger along the rim of her glass. "What sort of rules?"

"We had chores, everything from the upkeep of our rooms to taking care of our bikes, then later our cars. At our weekly 'academic accounting' meeting with dear-old-Dad, the twin with the highest GPA was declared that week's winner. The loser had to take care of all the combined chores by himself, with the winner supervising. Then Dad supervised *him,* so that if he didn't come down hard enough on the working twin, he was punished."

Lauren stared. Matthias had said his spiel without emotion, but she could barely hold hers back. It formed a lump of appalled sympathy in her throat that was thick enough to bring tears to her eyes. "I—I don't know what to say," she finally managed to choke out.

"We were forced into competition over sports, too. At our weekly meetings he would tally up who had scored the most points in soccer, basketball, lacrosse, whatever the particular sport of the season was. Whichever one of us had done the most for the team that week got a free pass."

She swallowed, hard. "From?"

"A three-page, single-spaced book report. The loser had to read from a selection of nonfiction titles—Machiavelli's *The Prince, The Art of War* by Sun-Tzu, current books penned by the superachieving CEOs of the day—and then sum it up in three pages that would pass the muster of our Donald Trump of a dad. After, of course, being graded on the essay by the higher-scoring twin."

Lauren could only state the obvious. "I suppose that didn't foster much brotherly love."

His response was flat. Cool. "After our mother died, the Barton house was devoid of love."

Okay. Wow. There was the getting-to-know-you-better chat and then there was the really getting-to-know-you-better chat. What her fiancé had just told her went a long way to explaining not only his workaholic ways, but his strained relationship with his twin. They'd been raised as warriors in opposing armies instead of brothers who could rely on each other for support.

When was the last time the man sitting two feet away had felt as if someone was on his side?

Without thinking, she scooted along the couch so that she could touch him. She couldn't help herself from wanting to make contact with him, skin to skin. Her hand found his strong forearm and she laid her fingers on it and stroked down toward his wrist, trying to tell him through touch what she wasn't sure she could—or should—say.

I'm here for you. We can be allies, not enemies.

Matthias looked down to her caressing fingers, then back up to her face. "Not that I'm complaining, mind you, but are you by any chance breaking one of your rules already, Lauren?"

She froze, then backed away from him. She was already breaking her rules! She was! How could she have forgotten so quickly how she wanted to limit their physical contact?

Matthias gave her a wry smile, as if he could read her mind. "Don't worry, sweetheart. As to where we're taking the attraction…well, that's all in your hands now, Lauren. As a matter of fact, 'hands' is the operative word here. I promise I won't lay one of mine on you unless you ask."

Oh, terrific, she thought, looking at the beautiful man who had just bared a part of himself to her. He wasn't going to lay one of his hands on her unless she asked.

Just what she was afraid of.

Five

An hour later, Luke still didn't know what had possessed him to spill about what had passed for "childhood" in the cutthroat Barton household. Uncomfortable with his own revelations, he'd jumped up from the couch as soon as he could and strode toward the kitchen.

"There's plenty of food in the freezer and fridge for dinner options," he'd called to Lauren, who'd stayed behind on the great room's couch. "I'll let you know when it's ready."

When he was ready to face her again.

Maybe she'd figured that out herself, because she left him alone to microwave another gourmet meal from Clearwater's, only venturing as far as the dining area to set their places. Smart girl, he thought, as he exited the kitchen with a plate in each hand. She'd put them at the two heads of the long table, leaving a safe distance between them.

He needed that space so that he could keep his mind on what he was doing here with her. He hadn't wanted to jeopardize it when they'd nearly bumped into Nathan and his mayor on the street that morning—he'd had to call his old friend with excuses that afternoon. He didn't want to jeopardize it now.

Their time together wasn't about Luke discussing his ruthless father's way of raising children. It wasn't about exploring the chemistry that she was so intent on making rules about. No, he'd encouraged her to stick around because this was about Matt. It was about how Luke could use this chance encounter with Lauren to get retribution for what Matt had done to him seven years before and for what he seemed to be preparing to do now.

As they finished the last bites of their meal, Luke looked down the length of the dining room table to study his dinner companion. What did Lauren know about what her father and Matt were planning? And what would it take for him to get it out of her?

"So," he said, pushing his plate away from the edge of the table. "How about a soak in the hot tub on the deck?"

Her gaze flew to his. "Um…"

"Warm water. Relaxing bubbles." The perfect location for him to worm from her the combined Conover-Barton intentions.

"I don't…a hot tub…"

From the alarmed expression on her face, he might

as well have suggested doing something X-rated in the middle of Main Street.

He shook his head, smiling a little. "I told you, everything—or anything—physical between us is up to you, Lauren. You can trust me."

"Well—"

"Or at least you can take this opportunity to find out exactly how trustworthy I am."

A smile twitched the corners of her lips. "Not a bad idea, but I didn't bring a bathing suit with me."

He shrugged. "Me neither. We'll skinny dip."

"I'm—"

"Chicken? There isn't any reason to be, you know. I won't turn the deck or hot tub lights on. We can slip outside in towels and slip into the water when the other person's eyes are closed."

"But—"

"You were all set to marry a Frenchman on the top of the Eiffel Tower but now you won't get into a Tahoe hot tub with your fiancé? Where's your sense of adventure, Lauren?"

She scowled at him, and for some reason it made him laugh. "You make it hard for a woman to say no," she complained.

He laughed again. "I take it that's a yes?"

And it was, though half an hour later he doubted his powers of persuasion. Not that she didn't scurry out to the deck wrapped in nothing more than a striped beach towel, but he was doubting the wisdom of what he'd persuaded her into in the first place. As promised, he'd left off the lights but, even with forested darkness surrounding the house, thanks to the moon her bare shoulders gleamed like the surface of a pearl and her blond hair stood out—a pale flame in the night.

He remembered her body beneath the robe, how it was as if it had been constructed to his exact specifications. Curvy breasts, curvy behind—dangerous, dangerous curves.

"Close your eyes," she ordered, approaching the side of the redwood tub.

It didn't matter that he was obedient. Even with his eyes screwed shut, he could imagine everything as he heard the soft plop of her towel dropping to the deck. She'd be naked now. And then he heard the quiet swish of the water and felt the way it lapped higher on his chest as she lowered herself inside the hot tub—calves, knees, thighs, hips, rosy nipples now disappearing from his fantasy view.

His body responded accordingly, part of him rising up as he imagined her dropping down into the wet, silky heat. Even though he knew the night would cover his reaction, he edged away from her on the hot-tub bench.

She exhaled a relaxed little sigh. "You can open your eyes now."

Maybe he shouldn't. Maybe he should keep them closed so he could concentrate on the information he hoped to get from her. *Don't think about her body!* he reminded himself. *Don't think about her wet, naked, curvy body!*

Think instead of saving Eagle Wireless.

And of retribution.

He cleared his throat and slipped a little deeper into the water as if he were unwinding, too. "So," he said, pretending the question was just an idle musing, "how involved are you in your father's company?"

"You mean Conover Industries?"

"Does he have more than one?"

"No." She released a wry laugh. "He needs to have a single company, I guess, if he's going to be as single-minded as he is about business."

"Mmm." Luke tried again for that idle-musing tone. "Does he talk about work at home? You know, about how the company's doing, possible new ventures, that sort of thing?"

"I don't listen when he does."

What? "Not ever?"

"If you think listening to my father drone on to the point of talking over everyone else—including his teenage daughter who wants to share about the new play she's in, or her new teacher, or her new passion for Web site design—is suitable or enjoyable, then you need to eat more meals with the Conover family."

"Ah… Well…"

"You see, in my opinion, the dinner conversation *chez* Conover is pretty much as appropriate as talking about my father and his company on a beautiful spring night in a heated hot tub instead of simply being quiet and appreciating the incredible stars overhead and the inky shadows of the trees around us."

Luke blinked.

If he wasn't wrong, she'd just told him to shut up.

To shut up and relax.

Then he remembered her remark during their exploration of Hunter's Landing that morning. *Haven't you heard of strolling?*

Apparently he was supposed to be "strolling" through this evening as well. Fine. Willing his legs not to fidget, he shook out his arms and raised his gaze. Okay. There were those stars she'd mentioned. That moon.

What the hell is my brother doing right now?

The question popped into his head and he saw spreadsheets instead of sky. He breathed in fire instead of fresh air.

Despite the heat of the water, his muscles went rigid. *If Matt ruins my Germany deal, I'm ruined.*

Luke jumped to his feet. Lauren let out a little shriek. Startled, he fell back to the bench. "God," he said. "You just scared the life out of me. What is it?"

"You. *You* scared *me.*"

"Huh?"

She made a vague gesture in his direction. "All of a sudden you stood up and you were, um, wet."

Wet and naked. Hell, he hadn't been thinking about his state of undress. He'd been thinking about his damn twin and then he'd been on his way to his cell phone and a plane ticket to Germany where he would wring Matt's neck.

But he couldn't do that. For the rest of the month, Luke couldn't leave this house, not when it was Hunter's last request.

Swallowing his frustrated groan, he tipped the back of his head against the rim of the tub and tried uncoiling the tension in his neck, his spine, the back of his legs. *Take it easy, Luke. Relax.*

"Are you all right?" Lauren asked.

"No." He grimaced at the clipped sound of his voice.

"Look, I know I invited you out here, but the truth is, I'm not so good at this relaxing stuff. I don't nap, I don't meditate. As far as I know, I don't even take deep breaths."

She laughed. "Is there anything I can do?"

He rolled his head toward her. The starlight caught in her eyes and they gleamed. *So pretty.* "Talk to me, Lauren. Otherwise, I think the silence might make me nuts."

"You just need to get used to it."

This time he didn't hold back his groan.

She laughed again. "All right, all right. What should I talk about? My father, or—"

"Kaitlyn," he said, surprising himself. "Tell me about your sister."

"Ah. Kaitlyn." Lauren wiggled on the bench, sliding a bit lower into the tub. She must have stretched out her legs, because the water feathered against his foot, letting him know she was only a toe or two away. "My infuriating, adorable and genius-IQ baby sister."

"Genius IQ?"

"Mensa genius IQ and then some." Lauren shifted again and this time he felt the brush of the bottom of her foot against the top of his.

He pretended not to notice.

"Kaitlyn terrifies my mother and father."

"But not you?"

"Oh, me, too, but when she points out their foibles and flaws, my parents can manage only to sputter and spit."

As he slid his heel along the slick bottom of the tub, his toes found the little bump of her ankle bone. He gave it a small nudge. "And what does Lauren do?"

"I humbly acknowledge she's right and promise to do better next time."

She went silent, so Luke nudged her again. "Don't leave me in suspense. What's her latest critique of your character?"

"Let's just say she's not fond of junior bridesmaid dresses."

Little sister Kaitlyn thought Lauren's marriage to him was a bad idea.

No. Her marriage to *Matt.*

The reminder annoyed him. "Maybe if the Conovers and the Bartons merge, I'll have to be listening to Kaitlyn myself. Does she have ambitions regarding your father's company?"

"She has ambitions to take over the world. Global peace for the masses and Justin Timberlake for all teenage girls." Her leg moved again and a silky swipe of calf met his own hair-roughened one. "But seriously, I can see her being the CEO of Conover in the not-so-distant future."

He stretched a little more in order to hook his foot around her delicate ankle. They were twined together, now, but it didn't appear to bother her. "What about you?"

"What about me what?"

Did she sound a little breathless? "Do you have any interest in getting involved in the family business?"

Her laugh was short. "You're kidding, right? My father wouldn't find use in Conover Industries for my skills in French and Spanish."

But what about German? Could she speak that, too? Luke remembered he was supposed to be digging for anything he could find about his brother's business instead of finding her sleek leg in the warm wetness. "Lauren—"

"You can't be surprised. I'm sure my father made it clear. The first and only time he's ever approved of me or anything I've done was when I agreed to marry Matthias Barton."

Lauren wished she'd never mentioned the word *marry*. It had sent Matthias catapulting from the hot tub with only a curt "Close your eyes" warning. While wrapping a towel around his hips—of course she'd watched through her eyelashes!—he'd mumbled something about bringing them back some wine before disappearing into the house.

She'd spooked him with the wedding talk, which was weird, because she'd come to the Hunter's Landing house spooked by the idea herself. Yet now…now the idea of being with him gave her an odd feeling of rightness. Odd, because she'd never sensed it on those other occasions when she'd been with him. But the feeling itself was familiar.

The day she'd met her freshman roommate in college, she'd known they were going to be friends for life.

Her senior year, within an hour of interning at the publishing company she still translated for, she'd understood at some cellular level that she'd found her place.

Did it work like that with the man one married?

And if it did—then why hadn't she known when she'd danced with Matthias at the Jewel Ball or when she'd passed him the basket of dinner rolls at her family's table?

Maybe it was her glimpses of all his wet muscles

that had turned the tide. Face it, both sides of his body were spectacular. He might be a workaholic, but some of those long hours must be spent working out. While the wide set of his shoulders might be genetic, it took effort to create the sleek round of muscles supporting them. And then there were his pecs—she'd never considered herself a connoisseur of a particular male body part, but she might have to change her own opinion of herself. Could be she was a chest girl after all.

Yes. After looking at those defined, yet not overdone plates of pectoral muscle gleaming with water in the moonlight, she'd definitely discovered their allure.

And she'd peeked at his butt as he was wrapping that towel around his hips. *Bad Lauren!* But she'd merely been checking out his shoulders from behind and then her gaze had coasted down all that wet skin toward his waist and from there it was just a little *whee!* of a slide to his cute, contoured backside.

So maybe that was it. Maybe her marriage *no* had been transformed into a marriage *maybe* by something as shallow as the way her fiancé looked wearing nothing but H_2O.

Except that didn't explain why she'd felt so drawn to him last night. How much she'd enjoyed breakfast and their walk that morning, even counting the way he'd exposed his hypercompetitive streak at The Game Palace. He'd laughed at himself about it and that kind of humorous self-deprecation held as much charm for her as his smile, as his interest in Kaitlyn, as his understanding that she didn't want to fall right into his bed without getting to know him better, engagement or no.

No engagement. That's what she'd wanted, but now

she didn't want to make *that* mistake either. Now she wanted to be with him.

And so where was he? Surely a simple bottle of wine wouldn't take this long?

A niggle of unease tickling her spine, she scrambled out of the hot tub and swiped up her towel. When he still didn't appear, she took herself and her terry cloth-wrapped body through the French doors. "Matthias?" she called out. "Everything okay?"

Their stemmed glasses were on the countertop in the kitchen along with a bottle opener. But no wine and no man. Recalling the location of the wine cellar from her earlier tour, Lauren headed in that direction.

Her bare feet were silent on the carpeted steps that descended to the lower level. A right turn took her into the small room lined with shelves stocked with bottles. A small table stood in the middle of the room and what looked like a merlot rested on one corner. It was clear that Matthias had forgotten all about it, his attention now focused on dozens of photographs fanned across the wooden surface.

She thought of the framed photos in the hallway upstairs. She hadn't done much more than glance at them enough to gather they were various shots of scruffy young men whom she presumed were the Samurai. She suspected these were more of the same.

Gripping the doorjamb, Lauren called softly in order not to startle him. "Matthias?"

Her fiancé didn't turn around. "He's right here," he said, tapping a photo.

"Hmm?" She ventured farther into the room. "That's a picture of you, you mean?"

He froze, then whirled around, his hands going wide as if he was trying to hide what he'd been inspecting. "Oh. Sorry. I left you out there, didn't I?"

Curious, of course, she drew closer to the table. "That's all right. What're you looking at?"

For a second he didn't move and she wondered why he was so protective of what lay on the table.

"What?" she said, trying to peer around him. "I didn't uncover you admiring your stash of secret black-mail material, did I?"

A ghost of a smile broke over his face. "Close. More college photos of the Seven Samurai. I stubbed my toe on the box."

It was beneath the table now, the white cardboard neatly labeled "Hunter-Samurai." She shifted her gaze to the top of the table. "May I look?"

She had the distinct feeling he wanted to refuse, but then he sidestepped to give her access.

"I'm not going to be shocked, am I?" she asked as she moved in.

He shrugged. "You tell me."

Even with his earlier admission about not doing well with relaxing, there was no missing the new, tighter tension in his body, just as there was no missing the lack of reason for it—at least from her first, cursory inspection of the photos. "Hmm," she said, peeping at Matthias through the corner of her lashes. "If I had to guess I would say you seven majored in beer, basketball and busty co-eds."

Truly, though, there was nothing she could see that would put him on edge. There were plenty of grins, some boozy, on the faces of young-faced college boys who posed with their buddies and some long-legged girls—was every female long-legged at the age of twenty?—in various combinations.

Matthias was in many of them, most often with a sandy-haired, good-looking boy with a buzz cut and a laugh in his eyes. His charisma came through paper, space and time. Lauren lifted a close-up of the smiling face. "Let me guess. Hunter?"

"Yeah." A corner of his mouth hitching up, Matthias took the photo from her hand. He ran his thumb along the edge. "Hunter. He could make an all-night study session an adventure. He'd set an alarm for every hour and when it went off he'd announce some crazy item we'd have to scavenge for in ten minutes or less. The quick break combined with the adrenaline rush would hone our focus for the next fifty minutes of studying."

The easy way he talked about the other young man told Lauren it wasn't memories of Hunter that had agitated him. She looked back at the photos, pushing some aside with her finger to reveal another, larger one, beneath.

And then it struck her, something she hadn't thought through during her cursory view of the photos upstairs. On the table were plenty of shots of a younger Matthias but, looking at this particular picture, she realized they might not all have really been of him. Because this photo showed two faces mugging for the camera. *Two identical faces.*

Of course he had a twin, Luke. But until this moment she hadn't thought to determine how closely they resembled each other. And now she knew. Picking up the photo to hold it closer, she confirmed her first thought. They looked exactly alike.

And in this picture, at least, they looked pleased to be in each other's company. From the corner of her eye, she noted Matthias was studying her face instead of the photo she held. She turned it his way. "Which one is you?"

He shrugged without looking at it. "Doesn't matter."

She shrugged, too. "I guess not. You both look equally…"

"Drunk?"

Her gaze shifted back. "I don't think so. There's a basketball in your hands and it appears you've just finished a hard game."

He nodded. "Hunter likely took that one then. We were a team in a huge three-man basketball tournament. We came out on top."

"You and your brother were a team?"

"With Hunter."

She pressed. "You and your brother were on the same side?"

"We seemed to be in college."

For those years, they'd somehow left behind that sick competition their father had fostered during their childhood. Had it been Hunter's influence, or just a natural brotherly love allowed to find the sunshine away from their father's presence?

"What happened after college?"

"You don't want to know about all that."

Like heck she didn't, particularly because her sudden shiver underscored the new cool tone in his voice. This was exactly the kind of thing she wanted to know all about.

"You're chilled," he said. "Let's go back to the hot tub."

She was chilled *and* naked. He was still just in a towel, too, and there was quite a bit of male muscle to admire. But it didn't stir her even one iota at the moment, not when the sort of nakedness she was interested in right now was the emotional kind—the kind a man shared with the woman who had promised to become his wife.

"What happened between you and your brother, Matthias?"

"Matthias," he muttered under his breath. "Damn. Matthias and Luke. Luke and Matthias. It might as well be Cain and Abel."

"Matthias—"

"Forget it, okay?"

"No. I—"

"I said, leave it alone." He strode toward the doorway. In a moment he would be gone.

The moment would be gone.

"Wait, wait. Just answer me this."

He paused in the doorway, his back still to her. "What?"

"Why? Why do you hate your brother?"

He didn't turn around to face her. But she didn't need to see his expression because she could hear the frigid anger in his voice. "It's because, God help me, he so often has what I want. Now leave it alone."

With that, he left *her* alone in the wine cellar. Alone and with one sure thought. She'd wanted to get to know him better and now she did. Now she knew that talk of his twin was off-limits.

With a sigh, Lauren left the wine and the photographs scattered on the table. Unfortunately, she suspected it was his relationship with his brother that her man needed to open up about most.

At 2:45 a.m., Lauren gave up on sleep. Her lightweight cotton-knit travel robe lay across the end of the bed and she slipped it over the matching nightgown and barefooted it downstairs. The house was silent and dark, but her fingers managed to find the kitchen light switch to flip it on.

"Huh!" A startled male grunt and a liquidy thud told her she wasn't alone. It took her a moment to blink past the fluorescent dazzle of the overhead fixture, but then she saw that Matthias stood at the sink, an empty glass in one hand. A half-gallon carton of milk had landed in the sink, but enough of it had geysered from the open top upon being dropped that there was a big puddle on floor at his feet.

"I'm sorry!" Lauren hurried forward. "Don't move or you'll track the milk all over the place."

With a wad of paper towels in hand, she knelt to soak up the liquid on the floor. "You didn't hurt yourself, did you?" she asked.

"I'll survive a milk bath," Matthias grumbled. "You surprised me, that's all."

"I'm sorry about that, too." She rose with the dripping paper towels and dropped them in the sink. "I couldn't sleep."

"Me neither."

What was the cause of *his* insomnia? "I'm sorry—"

"That's not your fault either," he answered, wiping off the sides of the carton with a wet sponge.

Reaching around him, Lauren wet clean towels then kneeled again to wipe the floor. As much as she regretted being the cause of the mess, she was glad for the opportunity to talk to him again after what had happened earlier. She didn't want the awkwardness of it lingering between them.

A swipe of dry cloths later, the floor was once again pristine. The used towels went in the garbage. "You're free to move now," she said to his back.

He turned to face her.

"Oh." She tore another towel off the roll. "Not quite done after all." Her arm reached out to wipe away the drops of milk that were sprinkled over his chest.

His bare chest. Revealed in all its lovely male perfection thanks to the low-slung pair of pajama pants he was wearing as his only sleep attire. The pants were really cute—a soft olive cotton with all-business pinstripes. All-business pinstripes that didn't appear the least bit Brooks Brothers when they were slung so low they were doing that whole mouth-drying, hormone-heating, hanging-by-the-hipbones thing.

Lauren realized she was standing there, staring.

And that he was staring at her staring.

And that the temperature in the room had turned so warm that the milk on his miles of bare chest had to be in danger of evaporating into latte steam. Clearing her throat, she reached farther to dab at his chest with the paper towel. At the touch, goose bumps broke out across his collarbone and she saw the centers of his copper-colored nipples tighten into hard points.

She swallowed her squeaky moan and tried breaking the sudden sexual tension with her usual MO—babbling.

"I really am sorry about surprising you in here, Matthias," she said, as she continued stroking spots on his skin. "And that you're having trouble sleeping. And then there's the milk that went on the floor, not to mention all over these gorgeous muscles on your hunky chest…"

Her voice petered out as the sound of her own words reached her brain. Her hand froze and her gaze dropped to their bare feet. "Oh, tell me I didn't just say out loud what I think I said out loud."

She felt his laugh through her fingers. "Lauren, Lauren, Lauren." His hand came up to cover hers and then he guided it lower so the towel bumped over the sculpted muscles of his abdomen.

Her fingers opened. The paper wad dropped to the floor. The tips of her fingers absorbed the heat of his skin and he drew them lower, lower. Now she felt the soft fur of the hair below his navel. Now her fingers grazed the waistband of his PJs.

His free hand at her chin, now he tipped up her mouth and looked into her eyes. More heat. And need.

And then that undeniable, oh-so-puzzling but oh-so-welcome feeling of rightness.

"Lauren," he said again, his thumb brushing over her bottom lip. "Didn't anyone ever tell you not to cry over spilled milk?"

Six

Didn't anyone ever tell you not to cry over spilled milk?

The words echoed in Lauren's mind as she looked up into her fiancé's face. Did that mean she shouldn't cry over broken rules, either?

In particular, the one regarding not falling into bed with Matthias until she got to know him better?

Spilled milk. Broken rules. The parallel between the two didn't make real sense, she could admit that, but nothing was making sense lately. Not the strength of this attraction she had to him and not the way it had suddenly come upon her the moment he'd opened the door to her on that rainy night.

"Oh, boy," she whispered, knowing she was in trouble. Her fingers curled, her nails scratching at his bare belly skin. She felt his muscles flinch and his cheeks hollowed as he sucked in a sudden breath. "Oh, boy."

"Oh, man," he corrected, with a faint smile. The hand he'd cupped over hers guided her palm a tad lower until she wrapped his rigid flesh. It twitched at her touch. "Oh, *man*."

Her mouth curved as his lips lowered. She couldn't help but smile into his kiss.

But it turned serious the instant her mouth parted and the tips of their tongues met. Heat rushed across the surface of her skin and she went on tiptoe to press harder against him. His wide hands splayed against her back and drew her nearer.

Her head fell back as she surrendered to his deepening kiss. His tongue plunged inside her mouth and she echoed the motion by sliding her hand down his shaft. His whole body stiffened in reaction and, after a pause, he withdrew his tongue in a slow, deliberate movement.

She mimicked the action by gliding her hand high again. He thrust inside her mouth, she stroked down. He groaned and, loving the sound, Lauren palmed his erection in a seductive caress.

On another sound of need, he tore his mouth from hers. "Witch," he whispered, his eyes glittering. "Beautiful witch."

Hauling in much-needed air, Lauren wondered if the oxygen would bring back her common sense—or at least her sense of caution. But both seemed to have fled for good—or at least for the night. She wanted this man. She wanted, wanted, wanted him.

His head bent again to kiss her cheek, the side of her neck, and then he tongued the whorls of her ear, making her shiver. "Beautiful witch, are you going to let me have you?"

More shivers trickled down her neck. Have her? Would she let herself be had?

She'd wanted to know him better before acting on her desire and the truth was, she did understand him more. Though she didn't know how deep they went, she was at least aware of some of his wounds. And then there was the fact that she was hurt, too. Three times she'd been rejected as she stood on the curb of lifelong commitment and she knew those rejections had affected her confidence in herself, in her femininity and her own appeal as a sexual being.

By giving in to this man who made her heart beat so fast and her blood run so hot, to this man whose own desire for her she was holding in the palm of her hand, wouldn't she be getting so much else back?

And it still felt so right.

If nothing else, Lauren decided, she could regard going to bed with Matthias as a test. Perhaps the "rightness" was just a trick of the mind to pretty up something as simple as lust. And when the lust was sated, then the "rightness" would disappear and she'd no longer be fooling herself about it being something so much more… Something maybe even worth marrying for.

He caught the lobe of her ear between his teeth. Her fingers flexed on his shaft. They both groaned.

His mouth found hers again. He parted her lips and plunged inside and she twined his tongue with hers and crowded against his body, rubbing his erection, rubbing her aching nipples against the hot, naked flesh of his chest.

One of his hands slid from her back to cover her breast. He squeezed and the pressure felt so sweet— oh, fine, *so right*—that she had to bury her face against his neck and ride out the tremors of reaction. Kissing her temple, her cheek, any place he could reach, he continued molding the soft flesh in his palm and used his other hand to pull away the fingers she had around his own straining flesh.

"Can't take it right now, honey," he said, placing her palm on the bare skin of his torso. "It's too early for the fireworks."

She lifted her face and linked her hands around his neck to draw down his mouth. "I'm seeing sparklers everywhere."

They shot into wild arcs of heat and light as they kissed again, a wet, deep kiss that was a whole Fourth of July show unto itself. She lost herself in it, lost herself in his taste and his strength, until his thumb grazed her nipple.

Then flames shot up around her. Her body jerked in his arms and he slid his other hand to the curve of her bottom while his fingers found that tight bud and made maddening circles around it. She jerked again, her hips butting up against his erection, tilting to make a place for it as desire caused a liquid rush between her thighs in preparation for him.

He pushed back, nudging against the notch of her body with the head of his penis. With only thin layers of cotton between them, he was able to insinuate himself between the petals of her sex, the tip of him discovering her sensitive kernel of nerves. She cried out, unable to hold back the sound, and he responded by rubbing there again.

"You like that, sweetheart?" he murmured, looking down into her eyes.

She could hardly breathe and her nerves were humming like a tuning fork. "I—I like you."

He smiled and then the hand on her bottom started drawing up the material of her robe and nightgown together. Cool air washed over the back of her knees and then the back of her thighs and she shivered again, overloaded with sensation. When he had the hem of her clothing in his fingers, he drew up his hand and held his fist at the small of her back.

That cool air now found her naked bottom.

Wet heat rushed between her legs again.

Then in a quick movement he dropped the robe and nightgown—his hand now beneath them. His big male palm now covering her round, bare bottom cheek. Goose bumps prickled over her skin.

"You ready for me, sweetheart?" he whispered.

Ready? How could that be a question? She drew his head down for another kiss. His hand reached between her legs and just as his tongue plunged into her mouth, a long finger slid into her body.

Lauren gasped, then softened against him, opening to his intrusion by hooking her ankle around the back of his calf.

"You *are* ready for me," he murmured against her mouth and there was no way to deny it, no reason to deny it, when he was stroking in and out of her wetness with his clever, clever finger.

Then two fingers. She shivered, sucking on his tongue because she loved the feeling of fullness. Of being open then filled by this beautiful, beautiful man.

It still felt so right.

He lifted his head, his gaze narrowed, a pronounced flush on his cheekbones. "Counter or comforter?"

His fingers were deep inside her body. The tip of his erection was pressed tight against the pulsing ache at the top of her sex. She had no idea what he was talking about and couldn't care less.

"You have to decide, Goldilocks," he said.

She shook her head. She'd decided minutes ago, hadn't she? It was time to ease her lust, to test that sense of rightness, to get over those three rejections that had battered her heart.

"On my bed or on the breakfast bar?"

His question startled a laugh out of her which turned into a tiny groan as it shifted her body against the sweet invasion of his fingers. "You don't have to make the choice sound so romantic," she said, smiling to let him know she was teasing.

"And you don't have to make me so crazy with wanting you that I'd cover you out in the cold, lonely rain if that was the only way I could have you."

That's when she realized the weather had turned again. She could hear the sound of raindrops pattering down and she shivered a little, remembering how frozen she'd been last night. "By a fire," Lauren said. "Take me by a fire."

"Then wait here," he replied, removing his touch so that she wanted to cry with the loss of it. "Wait here until I tell you that it's time for me to have you."

Have you. Cover you. Take me.

As she waited alone in the kitchen, trembling with wanting and anticipation, the phrases ran in a loop through her mind. *Have you. Cover you. Take me.*

Primal, man-woman words of possession.

And she was possessed by the idea of having him, too. Of having him in her body. Of having sex with this particular man who might be the last man in her life if they survived the test.

His voice reached her in the kitchen. "Lauren, come upstairs."

She didn't remember the journey from the hardwood floor to the carpeted steps. She didn't remember mounting them or how she knew to go into the master bedroom with its half-closed door.

It was as if she heard Matthias's voice and then she was in his bedroom—that decadent bedroom, now made even more decadent with the light from a fire burning in the fireplace and casting yellow, orange and red tongues of light across the rumpled bed.

He stood to one side, still in his low-slung pajama bottoms. Lauren felt the heat of his gaze and the heat of the fire and the heat from wearing too many clothes when all she wanted between the two of them was the palpable desire that filled the room.

Her gaze on his face, she loosened the tie of the sash of her robe. She shrugged and the material fell to her feet. As she stepped away from it, her hands rose to the spaghetti straps of her gown. She pushed them aside and stepped forward again after the nightwear shimmied down her naked skin.

And then she stood before her fiancé, offering him all she had.

The poleaxed look on his face made her smile.

Have you. Cover you. Take me.

That could work both ways and it surely seemed as if it was up to her to jumpstart the rest of the event, now that her man appeared lust-stunned by the sight of her. At least she thought he was lust-stunned...

Uncertainty licked a cold line down her spine. Maybe what had been feeling so right to her wasn't mutual. "Is there...is there something wrong with...with..."

"With what?" Matthias said, a frown flickering over his face.

And the word popped out, driven by anxiety. *"Me?"*

He laughed, low and sexy, and her uncertainty and anxiety were chased off by the seductive sound. "The only thing wrong with you is that you're too far away, sweetheart."

His arms reached out and swept her up against him. The contact of their naked torsos made her gasp, but then he muffled the sound with his mouth, taking her into a kiss that turned up the heat all over again.

He backed up and when he fell onto the bed, she fell onto his chest, breaking their joined mouths. She sucked in a breath. "Are you okay?"

Sifting his fingers through her hair to push it away from her forehead, he laughed again. "I'm the most okay I've been in years."

She smiled, but then it died as Matt circled her waist with his hands and lifted her up his body so that he could nuzzle the valley between her breasts. Her palms slid across his crisp dark hair and her fingernails bit into his scalp as he turned his head to catch her nipple in his mouth.

Her back arched into the delicious sensation. He curled his tongue against her, gentle and tender, then sucked hard with a raw, male sound of need coming from deep inside his throat. His sound of pleasure only added to the agony of almost unbearable pleasure that arrowed from her breast to her core.

His head shifted and he plucked at the wet nipple with his fingers as he gave her other breast that arousing attention with his mouth. Lauren could hear her shallow breathing and even when she closed her eyes she could still see the shadows and firelight in the room.

It was like the two of them, that darkness and those flames. Though there were still things they didn't know about each other in the shadowed corners of their souls, that didn't stop the fire from burning between them, from consuming her doubts, from lighting the way to a future that felt so…so…right.

Always so right.

Matthias flipped their positions. Suddenly she felt the sheets at her back and on top the hardness that was his sinew and muscle and bone. She spread her legs to make a place for him, but he ignored the invitation to draw back and stand beside the bed.

With half-closed eyes, she watched his hands go to the drawstring at his waist and she let her gaze drop down to the erection straining behind the cotton.

"So pretty," Matt said, his voice almost harsh.

Her gaze shifted to his face, its angles made even more stark and beautiful by the flicker of the light. He was studying her, his eyes tracking over her breasts and down her parted legs.

Instinct caused her to bring them together again.

"Don't," he said softly. "Don't hide anything from me. Please."

And because she wanted that, too, she slid her heels along the smooth cotton and held out her arms in her own plea. "Come to me."

He shucked his pants in one swift move, then reached into the drawer of the bedside table for a condom. She had the brief impression of thick strength and then he was off his feet and in her arms, his shaft nudging at her entrance even as he took her mouth in yet another devastating kiss.

Lauren twined her arms around his neck and tilted her hips, asking for all of him, and he leaned more of his weight into her, taking her body one inch at a time. She stretched around him in degrees, going from breathtakingly tight to deliciously full.

He lifted his head as he joined them that last little bit. Her eyes closed with the goodness of the completion.

"Don't," Matthias whispered to her. "Don't shut me out like that either."

Smiling, she lifted her lashes. "Doesn't it feel good?"

He rocked a little into the cradle of her body. "What do you think?"

"I think it feels…feels…"

"Just right, Goldilocks," he said. "Not too hot, not too cold, not too hard, not too soft. Just right."

And of course those were her exact thoughts. And of course to hear them from his lips, in his husky heavy-with-desire voice, only made her more certain that she was in the right place with the right man.

Finally.

She tilted her hips to take him deeper, and he groaned, his head falling back. Then he drew away from her, almost to the brink, before sliding forward again. Her muscles tightened to hold him there, it felt so wonderful, but he pulled back again before another slow glide of penetration.

It was a rhythm she tried to fight and yet didn't want to fight. It felt so good to be filled by him and yet she had to let him go for him to come back to her. Her legs wrapped around his strong hips and he found a different angle that made goose bumps break across her skin.

"Oooh," she moaned, as he dropped his head to place openmouthed kisses against her neck. "Please."

"Please what?" he whispered against her ear. "Please what?"

As he continued to stroke in and out of her body, Lauren couldn't think of what she wanted more than this, just this, the play of reflected flames on his wide, powerful chest, the gleam of fire in his eyes, the blissful joining as the two people that were Lauren and Matthias became a single, indivisible whole.

His mouth found one of her nipples again and her body responded by tightening on his. He groaned, and the rhythm altered as both their bodies drove harder toward climax.

"I'm afraid I don't deserve this," he whispered against her mouth.

"I do," she returned.

He half laughed, half groaned and then his hand crept between their bodies and he touched her there, right at the spot that pulsed like another heart.

Gasping, Lauren lifted into the touch and his fingers grazed her again. And again.

"Let me have you," he whispered. "Go over, Goldilocks. Go."

Let me have you.

And she did, shuddering against him, around him, taking his own climax into her body. *Take me.*

As the last of the tremors wracked both their bodies he collapsed over her, heart to heart. *Cover me.*

And oh, Lauren thought. Oh, yes. It still felt so right.

It was hard to regret a nanosecond of what had just occurred, Luke decided, with Lauren's cheek resting on his chest and her blond curls drifting across his shoulder.

Who was he kidding?

It was *impossible* to regret the way her curves had looked, lapped by the light from the fire. It was impossible to regret the way her kisses had burned, the way her breasts had felt cupped in his palms, the sweet little noises she'd made when he'd taken their hard peaks into his mouth.

Hell, even as sated as he was, just remembering that made his blood run south again.

He pressed his mouth against her temple. "Lauren, are you all right?"

"Mmm." She snuggled closer against his side. He smiled at the contented noise, surprised to realize that he felt exactly the same way as she sounded.

But the guilt should be stabbing at him, right?

"Are *you* okay, Matthias?"

Ah, there was that guilt, he thought, wincing. Matthias. She'd gone to bed with him, thinking he was Matt.

He stroked his palm over her soft curls, wondering if he would be able to look at himself in the mirror come morning. "I didn't plan this. I didn't mean for us to end up here tonight."

"I know."

The two words didn't absolve him, though. He finger-combed her hair away from her temple. "I intended to honor my word to you."

"You did honor your word. You promised that whatever happened between us would be up to me, and as you'll recall, I walked in here of my own free will."

There was a hint of annoyance in her voice and he smiled. "You took off your clothes of your own free will, too. I particularly liked that part."

She let out a soft snicker. "You should have seen your face. You looked like a cartoon character after being hit by a frying pan."

"Are you laughing at me?" He reached down to pinch her curvy little butt.

She yelped. "Yes." Then laughed as he pinched her again. "Ouch! That hurts."

Without feeling an ounce of contrition, he rubbed at the spot, reveling not only in the satiny sensation of her skin, but in the relaxing, intimate laughter. Had he ever before found this combination of humor and sex? Before Lauren, he wasn't even sure he remembered the last time he'd laughed with anyone about anything.

At the thought, the guilt-knife stabbed again. Deep. She'd given him herself, laughter, this unfamiliar sense of contentment, while he'd been pretending to be her fiancé.

"Still, Lauren, I can't help but think this shouldn't

have happened. You aren't sure about the engagement, and—"

Her warm fingers pressed against his mouth. "Let me tell you something, okay? Something important."

He nodded, and she drew her hand away from his lips.

"When I was a little girl, I remember asking my mother how I would know the man I should marry."

"And she said…"

"She said I shouldn't worry about it. That she and Daddy would know and then tell me when they found him."

Luke had a sudden flash of insight. "For some reason I'm thinking that Mom and Dad weren't the ones to single out the surfer, the mechanic or even Jacques Cousteau."

"Jean-Paul," she corrected, then sighed. "But yes, you're right. You're my first family-picked fiancé, and you'd also be right if you guessed that I'm not entirely comfortable with the idea, either."

"So…"

She shifted to stack her hands on his chest. Resting her chin on them, she gazed straight into his eyes. Her pale hair frothed wildly around her face, the fire lending it the colors of sunrise and sunset.

"So I'd like to take the engagement off the table for the moment, okay? Instead, can we just be two people enjoying each other's company and nothing more? Can we do that?"

"Yeah," he said slowly, aware he couldn't have asked for anything more, though he likely deserved so very much less. "We can do that."

"Good."

He couldn't help but smile at the new, carefree sound of her voice. He couldn't help but feel carefree himself—once again, so unfamiliar but so damn wonderful. With a twist, Luke took her under him again. "So why don't you let me start enjoying you again, Goldilocks, right this minute."

Seven

Lauren left her lover sleeping in the rumpled covers of his bed. She tiptoed back to her own room, showered, then dressed and tiptoed again, this time heading downstairs to make coffee as quietly as she could. Something told her that Matthias didn't often let himself sleep late and she wanted to give him the opportunity.

Even as she worried about wanting to give him too much.

As she measured out grounds and water, she noted the new look of her bare left hand. Before taking her shower, she'd removed her engagement ring and she intended to keep it off. Last night, once he'd started making guilty noises about breaking his promise to her, she'd needed to say something to get him off that track. But once she'd made her proposition—that their engagement was now off the table—it actually had made sense to her, as well. As right as things were still feeling between them—last night neither that nor lust had been burned out—it was way better to proceed with caution.

She wasn't going to think of Matthias and marriage in the same sentence for the rest of her stay.

As she poured herself a cup of coffee, from her purse sitting on the corner of the counter came the sound of her cell phone ringing. Upon flipping open the phone, she grinned at the tiny screen, then held the piece of equipment to her ear. "What's up, Katy can-do?"

Her little sister got right to the point. "Connie called. You're not in San Francisco. Is everything okay?"

"Oh." Lauren made a little face at the mention of her former college roommate. Though she'd been hazy about her arrival time at her best friend's condo, she should have called to say she was postponing the visit. "I'll phone and tell her I'm staying here in Tahoe for a while."

"With Matthias?"

Lauren hesitated. "Promise you won't say anything to Mom and Dad."

The Mensa-moppet let out a deep groan. "Nooooo. That doesn't sound good. You said you were going there to break things off with him."

"I know." Lauren worried her bottom lip. "Look, Katy, you've been very eager for me to end this. Do you think…do you really think he's a bad guy?"

God, she sounded like *she* was in junior high, but who else could she speak to about him? Her parents were prejudiced, obviously, and Connie hadn't met the man. And to be fair, aside from her fixation on Justin Timberlake, her little sister happened to be a good judge of character.

"I never said he's a bad guy," Kaitlyn said with a little giggle. "I think he's funny. Have you ever watched him trying to work his BlackBerry?"

Lauren frowned. As a matter of fact, she'd seen him take a call on it when they were walking beside the lake the day before. She didn't remember anything remarkable. "I don't get it."

Her sister giggled again. "It was ringing one time when he was over at our house and he didn't know what to do. He had the most befuddled expression on his face and his fingers kept punching buttons until he'd set the alarm so it was both buzzing and ringing at the same time. I thought he was going to throw it into the deep end of the pool until I grabbed it away."

"Well you must have been a good teacher, because he doesn't appear to have any trouble with it now."

"Really? He didn't seem like a very good pupil and he told me he relies on his assistant to work all things technical."

Though that wasn't consistent with what Lauren had observed herself, she shrugged it away and pressed her sister again. "But despite that, you truly like him?" she asked.

"As a husband for you?"

"No, no, no." Remember? She wasn't supposed to be thinking of Matthias and marriage in the same sentence. "Just as a…as a person."

"I told you what I think. Yes, I like him. But wait a

minute." Kaitlyn's voice lowered. "Lauren, are you having sex with him?"

"What?" Her voice rose and she tried to soften it as she strode out of the kitchen and farther away from the man sleeping upstairs. "That is none of your business."

"Why?"

Lauren shot a glance up the stairs to the second floor and scurried down the other set of steps that led to the lower level. In the wine cellar, she closed the door and leaned her shoulders against it. "Why what?"

"Why won't you tell me if you're having sex with Matthias?"

Her fingers pinched the bridge of her nose. "Hasn't Mom taught you not to ask questions of that kind?"

"Yes, but after your stay in Paris, I thought you might have lost some of your American puritanism."

Lauren closed her eyes. "It is not puritanical to refuse to discuss sex with one's thirteen-year-old little sister."

"Then how am I supposed to learn anything about it?"

"Like the rest of us," Lauren retorted. "When you're much, much older."

"Puritan," Katy muttered under her breath.

Lauren pinched the bridge of her nose again. Not that she was going to discuss this with her sister, but last night pretty much proved she was not, in any way, shape or form, a puritan. Sex with Matthias had been pretty spectacular, if she did say so herself, and her heart gave a little jump-skip thinking about indulging in those kind of fireworks for a lifetime. Imagine—

No. She wasn't supposed to be thinking of lifetimes with him.

"So does this mean I'm going to have to wear one of those grody junior bridesmaid dresses after all? Mom found this one that I could *maybe* live with. It's pale blue with a darker blue satin sash…"

Lauren's mind spun away. Kaitlyn would look so pretty in blue. She could see it now, her little sister in a tea-length dress. Lauren herself in something simple and white, with a low, scooped back that would look demure from the front but would give Matthias that same hit-by-a-frying-pan face when he—

With a silent groan, she pushed away from the door. She walked over to the table in the middle of the wine cellar, idly picking up a photo in order to replace in her mind that prohibited matrimonial image. It was the shot of the twins she'd studied last night and, in looking at those two identical faces, she was struck by a new resolve.

"I've got to go now, Katy," she said, already starting to sort the pictures into two piles. There was something she had to do.

The truth was, with or without the engagement ring, with or without her declaration that their wedding was off the table, there was no way she was going to be able to get the idea of marriage and the man upstairs separated in her mind. But she wasn't going to take the notion seriously yet, either. At least not until she understood more about the two so-similar men smiling at her from the stack of photographs in her hand.

* * *

From the angle of the sun in the room, Luke knew he'd slept past his usual 6 a.m. start. Turning his head, he inhaled Lauren's flowery scent on the empty pillow beside his and smiled. He didn't stretch, he didn't even move, he just lay against the soft sheets and let himself wallow in the unfamiliar combination of satiation and relaxation.

Contentment. Yeah, that's what it was called.

And he intended to hold on to it with both hands.

Luke closed his eyes and conjured up Hunter's laughing face and mischievous eyes. *Thanks.* Without his late friend's will, he wouldn't be here in this house.

With this woman.

Thinking of Lauren again got him up and out of bed and into the shower. Once dressed, he found himself whistling as he made his way downstairs.

He *whistled?* Who knew?

Grinning at his own surprise, he helped himself to coffee in the deserted kitchen and took a few moments to gaze out the window and into the verdant forest surrounding the house. He couldn't whistle and swallow coffee at the same time, but his lighthearted mood didn't die.

No wonder. A guilt-free night of great sex with a great woman.

Lauren had given him a free pass on the engagement issue, which in turn gave him freedom from the identity problem. *Can we just be two people enjoying each other's company and nothing more?* she'd asked. *Can we do that?*

Yeah, they could do that.

Luke topped off his mug and then went in search of the woman he very much enjoyed enjoying. But she wasn't in any of that level's living spaces and he knew she wasn't in any of the bedrooms. He wandered downstairs and didn't find her in the wine cellar or using the equipment in the home gym.

Worry took a small bite out of his good mood as he trotted back up the stairs. Pulling open the front door, he saw her car still sitting in the drive. All right, he thought, his disquiet abating.

She hadn't found him out. Surely if she'd discovered who he really was she would have either left him or left him for dead.

But Lauren was still here and he was still alive.

He was certain of that when he finally found her standing in the loft-level office space, her back to him. His heart gave a weird clunk in his chest as his gaze ran from the springy denseness of her blond curls to the heels of the suede boots on her feet. It took him only four silent strides to reach her, it took only a breath to set down his mug on the desk in front of her, it seemed only right to sweep away her hair and press his mouth against the scented skin at the back of her neck.

She gasped, then relaxed as his hands cupped her upper arms. When he lifted his mouth, she turned her head to smile at him over her shoulder. "Good morning."

He returned her sunny smile and caressed her with a stroke of his thumbs. "I woke up alone," he said, trying on a mock ferocious frown. "Maybe I should have tied you to the bed."

"Then who would have made the coffee?" she asked, nodding at the steaming mug he'd slid on the desk.

"There's that." He reached around her body for the hot beverage then held it to her lips as she turned to face him. "Want some?"

"Mmm." Her hands cupped his as she tilted it for a sip.

Luke found himself staring at the way her pretty lips parted and then at the glimpse of wet, pink tongue he saw between them. Her gaze jumped to his over the rim of the mug and he felt the tug on that thread of sexual tension that was, as usual, running between them.

It added a spicy little kick to the warm contentment still oozing through his veins. Maybe it was time they went back to bed. "Lauren. Sweetheart…" He smiled again and let her see the wicked intent in his eyes.

Her pupils flared and she edged back, knocking something off the desk. He bent to retrieve it, then froze as he glanced down at what was in his hand.

One of those college pictures. Matt and Luke, looking… His fingers tightened, crumpling the photo. Looking happy, the way he'd been feeling until two seconds ago.

"Why the hell do you have this up here?" he demanded, his voice harsh.

Lauren snatched the snapshot away from his brutal grip. "Look what you've done," she scolded, placing the photo facedown against her jean-covered thigh, trying to smooth it out from the back.

"You didn't answer the question."

She gestured behind her. "I thought I'd make a collage on the corkboard of some of the college photos. There are several in the hallway but I like these, too."

His gaze followed her gesture. The long desk sat

facing the wall and on that wall was a rectangle made of corkboard tiles already peppered with pushpins, convenient for holding a calendar, take-out menus, or a montage of pictures that were at least ten years old. And that were mostly of Luke and his brother.

Staring at them, he felt anger surge through his system, flushing away that whistle-inspiring happiness that had been inside him only minutes before.

Lauren touched the side of his face. "Don't look like that. I'm sorry if seeing them bothers you, but I thought…"

"You thought what?"

She linked her fingers with his. "I've told you about the bad exes. I thought maybe you could tell me about…about…"

He couldn't seem to wrench his gaze from yet another photo of him and his twin, this one freezing forever a moment with Matt balanced on Luke's shoulders, ready for some ridiculous dorm-wide chicken fight. They'd laughed their asses off…and together taken on all comers and won.

Lauren squeezed his hand. "Matthias?"

Luke started at the sound of his brother's name on her lips. He wanted to get away from those photos and from the damn memories. He wanted her to be in his arms and take all the old anger and frustration away. Drawing her closer against him, he slid his cheek down the side of her face. "What do you say we leave the past up here and find a more pleasant way to spend our present?"

Kissing her neck beneath her ear, he felt her shiver. As she pressed herself against him, the warmth of his previous mood returned, along with a quick spike of sexual heat when her mouth rose to kiss his.

"What happened between the two of you?" she said against his mouth.

Closing his eyes, he pushed her away from him and took a couple of steps back. "Don't."

"Matthias." Her voice was full of disappointment. "*Matthias*."

That other name jabbed at him like a sharpened stick. "Lauren—"

"Please, Matthias."

"All right, all right." He shoved both hands through his hair. "You're not going to leave it alone, are you? You're not going to leave *me* alone."

He crossed to the room's small sofa and dropped onto it. Maybe if he told her then they could go back to that quilt-covered bed and forget everything but each other. His fingers combed through his hair again.

"My father's will went like this…" he started, and then he told her about Samuel Sullivan Barton's last contest. About how whoever made a million dollars first inherited all the family holdings. About how Matt had won everything and left Luke with nothing.

"You mean you," Lauren said, her hand rubbing against his thigh. Somewhere during the telling, she had found her way beside him on the couch.

Shaking his head, he looked into her concerned, sympathetic face. "What did you say?"

"You said that you were left with nothing. But it was Luke who lost that last competition and you, Matthias, who won."

"Right." He nodded. "That's the way it was. Matt

won. Luke lost." Looking away from her face, his gaze found those damn photos again. Basketball. Chicken fights. There'd been a short time when the Barton brothers had been an unstoppable team.

To avoid the thought, he jumped to his feet. "Let's get out of here," he said, pulling her up. "We'll do anything you want. Lady's choice, I promise, as long as it involves the bathtub or the bed."

But she wasn't looking at him in a sexy or steamy way. There was a frown between her eyebrows and more questions on the tip of her tongue. To stymie them, he leaned down and kissed her, thrusting deep inside her mouth until she moaned and clung to his shoulders.

Yeah. That contentment was just around the corner.

But then she broke away from him and stepped back. "Matthias…"

Always damn Matt. "What?"

"There's one thing I don't understand. If you received all the family wealth thanks to the terms of your father's will, why are you and your brother still estranged?"

"What do you mean by that?"

"Once you took over the Barton holdings, didn't you offer your brother half?"

He stared at her. "That's not the way my father wanted it."

"So?" She crossed her arms over her chest. "Are you saying you *didn't* ask him to join you in running everything together?"

Damn it, why was she pressing him on this point! "Yes. Yes, I offered him half of everything. I offered him joint authority and…and he refused." Luke would never forget how angry he'd been at Matt that day. To think that his twin could act so generous by offering to share what he'd actually stolen from him!

"He refused?"

Damn right, Luke had refused. "Yes." He grabbed her hand and started drawing her toward the door. "How about I find us some soap bubbles?"

She dug in her heels. "The story still doesn't make sense. If you made the offer and he refused, why are the two of you still not on speaking terms? Surely you both realize that it was your father who put you into that competition and not each other?"

Luke dropped her hand and stalked to the window. He stared out through the trees at that beautiful blue lake, but no matter how stupendous the view, it couldn't make over the truth. "We don't speak because Luke thinks I cheated in order to become the winner. He…he believes I bribed a supplier to favor me instead of him."

There was a moment of stunned silence. "You wouldn't do such a thing!"

His head whipped toward her. "What makes you so sure?"

"It's obvious. Your father raised you brothers to win, and neither of you would be satisfied to achieve victory through some sort of dirty trick."

For a moment, a weird emotion churned inside Luke's belly. Doubt? *Neither of you would be satisfied to achieve victory through some sort of dirty trick.*

But she didn't know Matt as well as she thought. And she didn't know the details of the events that had occurred seven years before. Luke knew. Luke knew what his brother had done to him. Didn't he?

Neither of you would be satisfied to achieve victory through some sort of dirty trick.

The words looped through his head again. And then again.

Staring at Lauren's big, blue eyes and flushed-with-righteousness face, he couldn't forget how she'd leaped to the—correct—conclusion that Matt had offered up half his winnings. He couldn't forget how she'd instantly assumed Matt wasn't a cheater as well.

Luke couldn't help but remember that he was bamboozling her right now, by pretending to be the very man whom she was so eager to defend.

Images of the night before scattered like more snapshots in his mind. Lauren's eyes, wide and darkening, as she lifted her hand to daub the milk from his chest.

The look of her kiss-swollen mouth as she laughed when he demanded she decide between the bed and the breakfast bar.

Her perfect body, all pale curves, rosy nipples, blond curls as she let her nightgown drop to her feet.

Later, when she'd let him look his fill, taking in all the female enticement of her petaled sex between her splayed, satiny thighs. She'd blushed, but she'd opened to his gaze and opened to his body.

Luke's body, but she hadn't known that.

Maybe he should tell her. Explain. Reveal the whole ruse before it went any further. As Luke, he could woo her now. Win her this time as himself. Then there would be nothing to threaten the contentment he could find in her arms.

"Lauren…" He crossed the room to cup her cheek in the palm of his hand. She edged closer and nuzzled into his touch and her trust struck him like a blow. His voice lowered. "Sweet Lauren…"

At his hip, his BlackBerry buzzed. He grimaced at Lauren, who let go a little laugh.

"Is that a bumblebee," she said, making it obvious she could sense the vibration, "or would someone be happy to reach you?"

His hand was reluctant to let her go, but business instincts ran deep and when he checked the screen he knew he would have to take the call. "Excuse me," he said, stepping back. Then he brought the device to his ear and acknowledged his assistant. "Elaine? What do you need?"

"I've been talking to Ernst in Stuttgart."

The supplier Eagle Wireless had been in talks with. And if those talks were successful, they'd take Eagle a nest or two up in the world. If not… Muting the phone, he looked over at Lauren. "I'm going to take this call downstairs, okay? Will you excuse me for a few minutes?"

She shook her head. "You stay here. I'm going to the kitchen to see what I can do about breakfast."

"Did I mention I don't deserve you?"

On tiptoe, Lauren pressed her lips against the corner of his mouth. "Just what I like. A man with a debt to pay."

He watched her sashay out the door, then returned his attention to the phone call. "Elaine? What's up with Ernst?"

"He's chilly."

The European had never been a particularly cheerful sort. "Any idea why?"

"If I had to guess, I'd say he has a second suitor for those components we've been talking to him about."

His hand tightened on his BlackBerry. "Do you know who?"

"I have my guesses."

"Yeah," Luke said. "Me, too." Matt. Matt was in Germany. Luke had suspected it before and now it didn't take a huge leap to deduce that Matt was his rival in the deal with Ernst. Damn Matt.

Luke's eyes closed as tension tightened like a vise around his head. See? Lauren was wrong for leaping to his brother's defense. And though that was no surprise, it shocked the hell out of him how his brother's betrayal could still hurt. He didn't have to open his eyes to see those college photos once again. Remembering each one opened yet another old wound.

For a short time they'd been so close. Together with Matt, Luke had felt as if nothing could vanquish him. How he missed that.

Opening his eyes, he strode to his laptop, closed on one corner of the desk. Seating himself in the nearby leather chair, he rolled it under the desk at the same time that he pulled the computer toward him. "I'm going to book a flight to Germany."

"I thought you had to stay in the house."

Luke's fingers froze on the keys. "I'll think of something." He was going to have to say goodbye to Tahoe and goodbye to Lauren, too, but it couldn't be helped. "Business comes first."

"Unfortunately for both of us," Elaine said, "and I say 'both of us' because I know what kind of mood you'll be in when I tell you this and that my poor, tender ears will be forced to bear the brunt of your outrage and I'll have to go home to my loving family, deaf in my right ear and thus unable to fulfill my motherly and wifely duties because—"

"Spit it out." Luke braced, because Elaine was nearly as ambitious as he was, and if she said "unfortunate" then it truly was.

"Ernst is going to be incommunicado for the next week. He's attending a big family wedding in the north and will not be available to talk business or do business until he gets back."

Luke blew out a long breath. "Hell. A week?"

"A week."

A week for him to stew over how he was going to save the deal. A week for him to nurture his rage at his brother over the way he was trying to pull the rug out from under the feet of Eagle Wireless.

A week to be with Lauren.

As Matt, damn it. As Matt.

He wasn't going to renege on the revenge he was plotting on his brother, though. No way. Not now. If Matt wanted to be Luke's rival on the Ernst deal, then Luke would continue wooing Lauren just as he had been doing. In Matt's name.

She'd taken off her engagement ring, hadn't she? They were "just two people," not two engaged people any longer.

With that thought in mind, he could still be content with making her happy in bed while waiting for the even happier day when he could watch his brother's face as he learned Luke had had his fiancée first.

It wasn't so despicable, was it? He made her as satisfied in bed as she made him, he was sure of it.

And Lauren had said, after all, she liked a man with a debt to pay.

Luke had a hell of a disbursement to lay on Matt.

Eight

Days passed, and Lauren didn't manage to coax Matthias into talking about Luke again—and to be honest, she didn't try very hard, suspecting it would ruin what they'd found. Together, they'd created their own little world within the environs of the log-and-stone house and the tiny town of Hunter's Landing; she didn't want anything to pierce the bubble of what they'd made together. Anyway, they talked about nearly everything else. The places they'd traveled to, the places they wanted to travel to, the interesting characters they'd met in their lives.

Nothing occurred to change Lauren's opinion that Matthias was a workaholic who needed to learn to relax, though, and the forced vacation at Hunter's lodge was the perfect opportunity for him to take his pace down a notch or two or ten. While he complained about feeling lazy, they slept in every morning. And because he seemed to have never taken the time off in the last few years to see even the most popular movies, she managed to persuade him into slow, cozy afternoons and evenings in front of the plasma TV, making headway through the extensive DVD collection they'd discovered.

Shivering, laughing or tearing up at a Hollywood offering was all the sweeter from the warmth of her man's arms. He'd squeeze her tighter when she'd bury her face in his neck as the knife-wielding villain approached the unsuspecting hero. His eyes sparkled when a particular comedy tickled her funny bone. As he'd thumbed away her tears during the denouement of an excruciatingly tragic love story, her stomach had flipped at the expression of tenderness on his face.

"Sweetheart, it's just a movie," he'd said, wiping away yet another tear.

She'd sniffed. "Great love isn't 'just' anything."

Amusement had joined the affection in his gaze as he'd shaken his head. "I'll take your word for it, I guess, but I'm thinking the hero might feel better if he went back to work or at least went out for a couple of beers instead of moping around with his dead lover's moldy nightgowns."

"Back to work. Out for beers. Moldy nightgowns." She'd tried pushing him away, but he'd lifted her like a rag doll and placed her on top of his body so there was nothing for her to do but accept his kiss.

And wonder if she should worry that he didn't appear to believe in love.

Maybe he'd sensed her mood, because then he'd distracted her by issuing a challenge to yet another of their air-hockey rematches. They were quite the regulars at The Game Palace now. She liked the sense of fun the place was now giving Matthias and something of his competitive spirit had begun to rub off on her.

She was the current champion in the twelve-and-under age bracket. It was a feat she was embarrassingly proud of, even though she'd been allowed to compete against players less than half her age only because the younger contenders had stated with a pithy pity bordering on scorn that they would let her play against them because she was "only a girl."

Ha! Now the preteen set had reason to rue the day they'd said those words and she continued to take each and every opportunity she was offered to hone her skills in preparation for beating the big, bad champion of them all—Matthias.

Now, from across the air-hockey table in The Game Palace, he paused, mallet in hand. "I don't like that ruthless gleam in your eye. You used to play with this don't-hurt-me-because-I'm-cute look on your face. Now that's changed."

She wiggled her brows, then gave him her best gunslinger glare. "I don't have to settle for that namby-pamby passive-aggressive stuff any longer. I'm going to start doing things your way—straight up."

A funny expression crossed his face. "I take it you mean you're out to win?"

"Loser buys the lattes."

She was crowing thirty minutes later as they waited in line at Java & More. "I did it. I did it," she started, then paused. "You didn't let me win, did you? Promise you didn't let me win."

He shook his head. "I didn't let you win. Fair and square, you beat me, Goldilocks."

She bounced on her heels, thrilled at the idea. Maybe some would see it as a silly accomplishment, but there was a deeper meaning to it. There was. Her usual response to the kind of aggressive attitude Matt showed toward air hockey was to either find a less-than-straightforward way to fight or to back away altogether. This time, though, she'd held up her head and kept her gaze directly on the prize.

From the corner of her eye, she sent a sidelong glance at Matthias. It had helped that he'd seemed distracted during the game. Though she could admit that, too, it didn't change the fact that she'd learned something from the win. And from him.

Spinning his way, she put her hand on his arm. "Hey."

He looked down at her, his gaze quizzical. "Hey, what?"

"You're good for me."

His muscles went rigid under her hand. "Lauren—"

"What can I get you?" the person at the counter asked.

They both looked up, startled to find themselves at the head of the line. "A medium coffee for me," Matthias answered, "and for Lauren…"

"Lauren?" The man on the other side of the counter blinked, then his gaze switched from Matt to her. He had sun-bleached blond ringlets that hung raggedly to his shoulders and bright blue eyes in a walnut-tan face. "Is that you, Lauren Conover?"

As she looked, really looked at the barista, heat flooded her face and she felt a distinct, needle-like poke. Ouch, Lauren thought, wincing. Ouch and damn. Her happy little bubble had just been pricked.

Beside her, Matthias cleared his throat.

Okay, that was her cue. She should say something. Do something.

Make introductions? Haul off and slap the guy who was supposed to be making their coffees? Curl up and die due to sudden onset of old humiliation?

As the silence stretched longer, Matthias's left hand curled around the back of her neck. His right stretched across the counter. "Matthias Barton, Lauren's…fiancé."

The barista shuffled his feet even as he shook hands. "Uh, Trevor Clark, Lauren's…first fiancé."

The shame of rejection flamed through her again, as hot as it had on the day she'd discovered he'd left on their honeymoon trip without her. She'd been in her bedroom when his note arrived, trying on her grass skirt which rustled every time she moved like the sound of a rodent running through weeds. Knowing it was going to make her mother nuts, she'd been smiling at her reflection in the mirror as Kaitlyn came in to deliver the sheet of paper bearing Trevor's nearly indecipherable scrawl.

For a few moments Lauren had thought he was suggesting they streak at their wedding ceremony. After squinting and making allowances for spelling errors, it became clear he was breaking it off. She could still feel the texture of the paper against her fingers. She could still remember the gossipy whisper of her skirt's grass fronds as she'd dropped to her bed. The guest list had been small, but gifts had already arrived and she could still remember each burning tear spilled as she'd repackaged for return every ten-speed blender and every gleaming set of chef's knives.

Alone.

Unwanted.

Unloved.

Now Trevor turned away to get the drinks and, mortification still coursing through her, Lauren couldn't think what to do next. She tried pretending she wasn't in the shop. Would that work? Was it possible to make believe she and Matthias were back at the house on the couch, in their just-the-two-of-us little world and that this embarrassing encounter wasn't happening?

Except the other half of "just-the-two-of-us" was squeezing her neck and bending close to peer into her eyes. "Are you all right?" His voice was quiet. Kind. Concerned.

She wasn't all right. Not only was it more-than-awkward to come face-to-face with the first man to dump her, but…but… Though a few days ago she'd wanted Matthias to know all about her failed engagements to make it clear what a bad bet she was when it came to marriage, things had changed since then. Now she definitely didn't want fiancé number four contemplating for even two seconds why she hadn't been able to please even a shaggy-haired coffee counter-person.

The only halfway decent option was to get the two

of them out of Java & More and back to the bubble ASAP. When Trevor returned with the drinks, she made to snatch them out of his hands. Who would guess that he'd choose to hold on to them when he hadn't been inclined to keep her all those years ago?

The grim set to his mouth was as tenacious as his grip on the coffees. "Look. I really should explain…" Trevor started.

"No need." On her end, Lauren tugged on the drinks, hard enough to burp a froth of foam from the sippy hole on the plastic top of her latte. Maybe if she pulled harder it would spew enough hot coffee to force Trevor into letting go. Her fingers tightened.

Another set of hands took over the paper cups. A warm chest pressed against her back. "I've got them, Goldilocks," Matthias said. "Let go, baby."

Baby. He'd never called her that before. It sounded sexy. Like a name a man would use for a woman who pleased him in bed. It sounded intimate. Like the way a man would talk to the woman he wouldn't mind keeping around for the rest of his life. Some of her humiliation leached away as her fingers loosened and then her hands dropped to her sides. Matt remained a warm presence behind her.

"Now—Trevor, was it?" he said. "What did you have to say to my wife-to-be?"

At the question, Lauren wanted to duck away, or at least close her eyes and again try that pretend-she-wasn't-in-the-room technique, but with Matthias at her back, she had nowhere to go. Make-believe wasn't working, either. The only consolation she had was that

Trevor looked more miserable than she felt. His gaze flicked to Matthias, then back to her.

"Lauren, I—I've felt guilty about it for years." He pushed his corkscrew curls over his shoulders. "I shouldn't have run off on you like that. With such a lame note and—"

"And with those trip tickets that Lauren had paid for herself?" Matthias sounded so polite.

Still, Trevor's face flushed an unbecoming red against the streaky-blond of his hair. "I'll pay you back someday, I swear. I don't make all that much right now, but I did okay as a ski instructor last winter. Maybe if I get the kayaking job this summer."

As he continued talking, his promises sounded as lame as that note he'd left behind and Lauren didn't know how to respond. Once upon a time Trevor had been the love of her life, and now he just seemed sort of...

"Pathetic," Matthias remarked as they finally exited Java & More. "My God. If this is an example of the kind of man you wanted to marry I'm starting to wonder if all your previous choices were simply a way of rebelling against parents. You certainly weren't thinking with your head. What did you ever see in that goofy, overgrown Peter Pan?"

"I loved him!" Lauren heard herself snap back. "He...he was a free spirit."

"Freeloader, you mean. Did you catch on to the part where he's living with some girl whose daddy owns a local resort?"

"Yes." Her voice sounded glum.

There was a moment of tense silence, then he

wrapped his hand around her arm and swung her to face him. "Tell me you're not still in love with him."

In love with Trevor? Lauren stared off into the distance. Of course she'd been in love with Trevor once, but it was hard to exactly recapture the feeling. It was much easier to remember the grass skirt, the embarrassment of rejection and how relieved her parents had been that she wasn't marrying a man—a boy— with such a distinct lack of prospects and ambition.

Now she looked up at *this* fiancé, noting the expression of irritation on his face. Because he was mad at her first fiancé *for* her, she realized. He'd given Trevor the icy poke about cashing in on the honeymoon, even as he'd stood behind her, a warm and solid presence.

Warm and solid. That described Matthias to a *T*, except it didn't take into account hot and sexy. And sweet and fun, she added, remembering all the sweet kisses as they lay laughing together on the couch and all the sweet moments she'd spent watching his face relaxed, finally, in sleep.

All at once, that bubble they'd been living in—the one she'd thought seeing Trevor had popped—was back. It seemed to invade her chest now, though, filling her so full that her heart crowded toward her throat and her stomach was flattened like a pancake. But then she realized the bubble *was* her heart and it was growing, taking up every inch of space it could find inside of her, because…because love took up a lot of room.

Love.

Swallowing hard, she gazed, helpless, into the dark eyes of the man her parents had picked for her.

"Well?" he demanded.

She swallowed again. Was there a question on the table? "Well what?" It came out a squeaky whisper, her voice box compressed by that unstoppable emotion getting bigger inside of her.

"Do you still love Trevor?"

"No!" Not him. There wasn't room for any other man in her mind, body or heart but Matthias. Yes, there was no doubt she was in love with him. This man.

The one whose ring she'd removed from her finger.

During the past few days, Luke had become accustomed to Lauren's moods. He knew what made her laugh and what made her sigh. He knew what she wanted when their eyes would suddenly meet across a table, a room, the mattress of the bed they'd been sharing.

He liked her moods. Her playfulness amused and distracted him during this period of forced inactivity. When he started stewing over his brother's machinations or when he experienced a resurgence of guilt over playing Matt, they faded away under his new preoccupation with the expressive curve of her lips or the wink of the dimple in her left cheek when she laughed. He found her sentimental side to be excessively girlie, sure, but a romantic movie could make her melt in his arms and who could find fault in that?

She'd become a damn good air-hockey player. Which would have been only a more amusing distraction if she hadn't spooked the hell out of him after their latest match by saying, *You're good for me.*

Good God. *You're good for me,* she'd declared.

He knew that wasn't true.

Luke wasn't any better for her than that loser Trevor who'd left her at the altar.

But she didn't know that, though he couldn't figure out another reason why she'd so suddenly be giving him the silent treatment. All the way back to the house from Java & More, she'd been like a ghost beside him in the passenger seat. Ghost wasn't one of Lauren's regular moods.

He unlocked the front door and she drifted in ahead of him, still surrounded by that unusual quiet.

Why?

She'd claimed to no longer be in love with Trevor, but...

"Lauren." His voice sounded harsh to his own ears.

"Hmm?" She kept drifting ahead of him.

It made him nuts; just as he thought he understood her, now he couldn't read what was going on inside her blond head. And his frustration with that only made him more nuts.

When it came to relationships, he never looked deep. He never cared too much.

Yet now he couldn't help thinking about which wheels were turning in Lauren's mind.

Yet now he couldn't help worrying about how this was all going to end up.

Yet now he couldn't help wondering why the hell he'd gotten himself into such a predicament.

She turned her head to look at him through her incredible lake-blue eyes. Her blond curls floated back and he thought, suddenly, of that fantasy woman he'd dreamed up on his first day in Hunter's house. He'd gotten all the outside specifications right, but he hadn't realized how much there could be on the inside. Warmth. Humor. That refreshing honesty that was like a deep breath of air he never could seem to take.

His hand rubbed against the center of his chest.

She frowned. "Did you need something?" she asked.

"No." He couldn't say it fast enough.

"Okay. I'm going to take a bath." She headed for the stairs without another look.

Which was good, he told himself. Without her around, he could let go of the worrying and the wondering. The examining and the analyzing. Maybe he'd turn on the TV. Find ESPN. An old Western. Lauren always turned up her cute nose to those.

He could lose himself in the tube and turn off this uncharacteristic bend to his mind.

Throwing himself on the couch seemed to help. He stretched out and reached for the remote. Any moment now, he'd be thinking of nothing at all as he surfed endless waves of brain-fogging television.

Good. A rerun of the game show, *Jeopardy!*.

Bad. The first category: "Sexy Blondes."

What was his sexy blond thinking right now?

Why had she been so quiet?

Clicking off the TV, he popped up from the couch. There had to be some way of redirecting his brain from focusing on her. From focusing on *anything*. Luke Barton only gave this kind of single-minded attention to work.

Never to women.

At one end of the dining-room table, they'd dumped out the contents of box holding a thousand-piece jigsaw puzzle. Now, he fiddled with the loose pieces and started sorting all those with straight edges.

Lauren, most likely, would make fun of this orderly method. She'd want to do it the wild way, he guessed, by blindly choosing one cardboard bit and then scrambling through the 999 other choices to find it a partner.

She'd definitely want to do it the wild way.

Luke pressed the heels of his hands into his eyes, trying to dispel the images those words dealt in his mind. He didn't want to be thinking of her.

He didn't want to be thinking of what she was thinking.

Of what she was doing.

She was taking a bath, a voice inside recalled for him.

Hell. Reminded of that, how could he possibly have anything *but* her at the forefront of his mind?

And then he could think of only one logical way to shut down his busy brain.

He took the stairs two at a time.

The flowery scent of the steam curled from under the door in the master bath and yanked him forward as if a hand had grabbed him by the neck of his shirt. Beneath his fingers, the knob turned without a sound.

At the sight that greeted him on the other side of the door he got exactly what he wanted…a sight that knocked everything out of his head.

Lauren in nothing but gleaming skin and soap bubbles.

Her head whipped around to face him. Her forearm crossed over her breasts. The warm-temperature flush on her face deepened. "Is everything all right?"

"No." He stalked closer. "I need…"

Her eyebrows drew together. "What?"

What was he talking about? Luke didn't need anything. Except mindlessness. Except sex, which would drive away all that he'd suffered today.

You're good for me.

Of course I'm not in love with Trevor.

If he knew the first wasn't true, how could he possibly believe the second?

"What do you need?" she asked, drawing back against the side of the tub as he came even closer.

His nostrils flared as he took in another breath of the scented water. He could almost taste her skin on his tongue.

He *had* to taste her skin on his tongue.

His fingers snagged the nearby towel, and he stretched it between his two hands. "Hop out now."

Her gaze jumped to his and *phttt,* a match struck and lit that ever-ready fuse between them. He saw Lauren swallow hard, but he didn't retreat at that sign of nerves. It was too important that they get body-to-body right now so that he could turn off his mind.

You're good for me.

Of course I'm not in love with Trevor.

One of her hands gripped the side of the tub and she pushed herself to her feet. Rivulets of water ran down her sides. Clusters of bubbles the size of cotton balls dotted her pink, naked skin.

Luke watched, fascinated, as one group skated down her belly to pause in the wet curls of her sex. She was blond and pink there, too, and so tantalizing that hunger gnawed at him. He had to have her.

As if he was pulling her on a string, she lifted one leg and stepped out of the tub, giving him a quick glimpse of the heaven between her legs before she was hidden behind the huge bath towel.

He wrapped his arms around her, encasing her in terry cloth. She looked up at him, a faint frown on her face. "I wanted some time alone to think."

"Oh, baby, bad idea."

"You wouldn't go away if I asked you to?"

He inhaled her sweet, sweet scent. "Are you asking me to?"

The answer was in her eyes, in the flare of the flame rising between them as that fuse continued to burn. Wrapped in the towel, she was easy to pick up and carry toward the bed.

She was easy to unwrap there, too, the damp ends of her hair making dark trails against the pale pillowcase. He stared down at all her bath-flushed skin and her scent rose around him as if he was rolling in a rain-dampened, flower-strewn field. It filled his head so that he was thinking only of Lauren, of her luscious skin, of the heat that he could feel radiating from her flesh as he crawled between her legs.

"You're still dressed," she whispered.

"You're not." He licked across her belly button.

Her stomach muscles jittered and he saw her pupils start to dilate. "I think—"

"Don't," he admonished, sipping a stray drop of water that was poised on one of her ribs. "Don't think."

No thinking. This was time for touching, caressing, tasting. This was time for easy, breezy sex.

His palms found her breasts. Her tight nipples poked against them as his mouth opened on the side of her neck. She made a little sound—protest and plea both at once—and he knew exactly how she felt. He sensed everything she was feeling through her shivers and her moans. Through the way her body twisted toward his mouth and twisted into his touch.

He sensed every unspoken word.

Her hips were lifting against his as the silent words clamored in his ears. She was rubbing against his jeans, probably abrading that delicate skin just inside her hipbones and, to spare her hurt, he lifted away despite another sweet yet muffled sound of desire. He calmed her by kissing down her belly and, yes, finding the redness where denim had scraped her delicate skin. With his tongue, he took a moment to soothe the marks and then drew lower, found her center, opened wide her satiny thighs.

She was blushing here, too, all pink and swollen and so inviting that his heart slammed against his chest, knocking loudly to make sure that Luke knew it was time to open this door.

He had to have her here, too.

She gasped at the first touch of his tongue. Her fingers twisted in his hair, but he could hardly feel it, overwhelmed as he was by the sweet, creamy taste of her in his mouth. Heat poured off her skin as he held her open to his feast and his mind spun away as her tension twisted higher. He could feel it through his hands, hear it in her breathless pleas, urge it on with the insistent *bam-bam-bam* rhythm of his heart.

He gave himself up to serving her desire, let it take control of him so that nothing else could intrude. There were no bothersome thoughts, no nagging worries, nothing but Lauren, her skin, her passion, the sound of her crying out in orgasm as his tongue stroked her to paradise.

Still shaking with the aftereffects, she pulled him up to her, her hands insistent now as she yanked at his shirt and pulled at the buttons of his fly. He shoved aside what was necessary, fumbled with a condom, then slid inside all her soft, clutching heat. His eyes closed and he threw back his head at the exquisite goodness of it.

As he began to move, again there were no thoughts, no recriminations, no wondering about feelings or future. Yes. Yes. There was only this sensation. The sensation of Lauren in his arms. Being in Lauren. A puzzle piece and its partner.

When he didn't think he'd survive the flaming pleasure of her body a second longer, she tilted her hips and took him even deeper. Made him helpless to the rocking rhythm they'd begun. Then, with one sharp jolt of bliss, pleasure sank like fangs and dragged him under.

He hoped he'd drown in her.

Somehow though, minutes later, he discovered he'd survived. Lauren was cuddled against his chest, her body as boneless as his seemed to be.

One of her fingers could still move, however, and she was using the tip to draw idle yet intricate patterns on his chest. A maze, he decided, and he let himself get lost in it, his brain still unengaged, just as he'd intended.

"Why did Hunter do it?" Lauren asked, her breath tickling the sensitive flesh at his collarbone.

Luke rubbed his chin against the top of her head. "Hmm?"

"Why did Hunter set up these month-long visits for the Samurai?"

Luke didn't plan his answer ahead of time. He still wasn't thinking. He still didn't want to think. "Because we're now in our thirties? Maybe he figured we'd need something at this time in our lives."

She stacked her hands on top of his beating heart and studied his face. "Well? *Did* you need something?"

"Yeah," he heard himself answer. "I needed you."

And those weren't thinking words. They were just the truth.

Hell.

Nine

It was dawn and Luke couldn't sleep. It was just like the old days—the days before he'd come to Lake Tahoe, when he was constantly revved. Then, he'd always been energized about his work, about making a buck, about proving himself to be a success without needing anyone or anything to back him up.

Now, and all during the night, his mind had flitted between two separate subjects, first picking up one, then the other, figuratively fingering each like pieces of that jigsaw puzzle. His brother, Matt. His lover, Lauren.

Leaving the second focus of his thoughts asleep in bed, he retrieved the box of college photos from the wine cellar and carted them into the kitchen. With the overhead light switched on and the coffee starting to drip, he took a breath and flipped open the cardboard flaps.

His own face stared back up at him. Times two. Lauren had dismantled her collage on the corkboard after he'd told her about the situation between himself and his twin. The photos of Matt and Luke were on top of all the others.

He drew a fistful out and fanned them on the table like a large hand of cards.

When partnered with Matt, he'd always come up a winner.

That's what he saw in the images caught on Hunter's film. Twins, identical enough that he couldn't pick himself out in most of the shots. Each face smiling, triumphant in good health, good spirits, in...brotherhood.

Had it been Hunter's magic that had brought them together during those years? Or a genuine feeling of kinship?

If it had been authentic, how could their father's will have destroyed it?

But the stipulation in their father's will hadn't destroyed it. Matt had. Matt had double-crossed Luke in order to make that first million.

Your father raised you brothers to win, and neither of you would be satisfied to achieve victory through some sort of dirty trick.

Lauren's words. Lauren.

Now he stared at the photos on the table, unseeing, his thoughts shifting to the woman sleeping upstairs in his bed. Without the request in Hunter's will, he wouldn't have taken a weekend, let alone a month, away from work. Yes, he dated when someone striking passed through his world, and he could find willing bed partners when that urge struck as well, but he'd never taken the time to really get familiar with a woman.

To know her favorite kind of movie. How she liked her morning coffee and how that was different than how she liked her evening coffee. The silly grin she wore when she caught him staring at her.

He'd never before found himself interested in the how and the why a woman wound up with three former fiancés and zero wedding bands.

He sat back in his chair, his mind turning things again, trying to understand how the pieces fit. Lauren. Matt.

Matt. Lauren.

A knock on the kitchen door jerked him from his reverie. He looked up from the photos and out the mullioned windows of the Dutch door. His reflection peered back at him.

Startled, Luke jumped, then his surprise ebbed away as the door handle turned and he realized it was Matt, not his own ghost, who was walking into the kitchen.

"Bro," his brother said. "Long time no see."

Luke shot to his feet and leaned against the table, using the shield of his body to hide the old photos from his twin. The last thing he needed was Matt supposing he was sentimental. When it came to his brother, he wasn't going to be stupid enough to reveal any weakness like that. "What the hell are you doing here?"

His twin sauntered over to the counter where he helped himself to a mug of coffee. "I thought I'd check in. See if you needed anything." His gaze circled the room, brushing along the granite countertops and the gleaming stainless-steel appliances. "Hunter did it up right, if the outside of the place and the inside of this kitchen are anything to judge by."

Luke crossed his arms over his chest. "You'll be comfortable enough when it's your month. Now go away until then."

Matt leaned against the counter, mimicking Luke's pose against the table. His head tilted. "You're looking fine, too. Rested."

"There's not much to do here but rest."

"It's more than that," Matt said. "I can't quite put my finger on it, but…"

"But I suppose your assessment of my appearance can be excused from your usual razor-sharpness due to the fact that we haven't seen each other in—how long?"

"Well, we did run into each other last year in that parking garage by the opera house. We both had tickets to…"

"Wagner," they said as one.

"God spare me," came out in tandem as well.

And then they were grinning at each other.

Their smiles clicked off at the same moment, too, as if simultaneously recalling their long-standing enmity.

Matt looked away. "Your date was stunning," he offered.

"Yours, too," Luke replied. "The woman I was with—"

He halted, as he suddenly thought of the woman he was with right now. The woman upstairs, sleeping like an angel in his bed.

Matt's fiancée, Lauren.

Matt and Lauren, two pieces of a puzzle that he definitely didn't want to link up today.

Setting his jaw, he pushed away from the table and headed for the kitchen door. "While it's been so much fun catching up," he said, "now it's time for you to go."

But his brother's gaze had caught on the photographs that Luke had been concealing. His mug firmly in hand, Matt walked toward the table instead of to the door that Luke was pointedly pulling open.

His brother lifted one of the snapshots off the table to study it. "Where'd all that go?" he murmured, turning the photo Luke's way. "You and me laughing together?"

"It went to hell, exactly where I'm wishing you right now," Luke answered, narrowing his eyes at the man who had promised to marry *his* Lauren. He couldn't get it out of his head, the image of her walking down the aisle and into the arms of the one man who always snatched away what Luke wanted. Their father's approval. The family wealth. The woman sleeping upstairs. "Time to leave, Matt."

"Lunkhead, for the last time, I didn't do a single damn thing to you, all right? I know you believe I somehow messed with your chances to win the Barton holdings, but I didn't. And it was *you* who refused your half later."

Luke didn't have time to get into this. There was a tick-tick-tick clicking away in the back of his brain, reminding him that any second Lauren could awaken, smell the coffee and head downstairs to find some...and him.

Two of him.

"Get out, Matt."

His brother appeared to grow roots that sunk into the slick surface of the kitchen floor. "Not until we get to the bottom of this. I'm damn sick of your false accusations and your bitter recriminations hanging over my head."

Anger tightened Luke's chest. False? Bitter? How could his brother dismiss his grievances like that? Still, it wasn't the time—there wasn't time—to hash it out with Matt. His fingers curled into fists and he jerked his head toward the open doorway. "I'm asking you to go."

Matt was shaking his head as a female voice floated down the stairs. "I woke up to an empty bed. Is my favorite man in all the world already up and making my favorite beverage in all the universe?"

Oh, God. Every muscle in Luke's body cramped to charley-horse tightness. *No. Not now.*

He remembered wanting to watch his brother's face when Matt realized Luke had Lauren first. He remembered rationalizing how fitting that would be, how it wouldn't be hurting anyone, not really, except the bastard who had delivered Luke that body blow by cheating him all those years ago.

But he'd never imagined the look on Lauren's face when she found out what he'd done. And he didn't want to see it now. Not until he figured out a way he could explain it to her that made sense—and made him look less like the villain he was suddenly feeling himself to be.

Frozen by his own body and seconds away from disaster, a desperate Luke sent an unspoken message to his twin. It had worked in the old days. The good old days, when they were a team. Real brothers. Maybe it would work now, as long as Matt hadn't recognized Lauren's voice.

Please God Matt hadn't recognized Lauren's voice. *Do what I ask, bro,* Luke silently urged his brother. He managed to jerk his head once more toward the door. *Please.*

Apparently Matt didn't realize who the woman in the house was—and apparently he still had some decency left. It surprised the hell out of Luke, but with a quick nod, his brother set down his mug then strode toward the door.

Luke released the breath he was holding as his twin, with a two-fingered salute, stepped over the threshold.

All right. Crisis averted.

Then Lauren's voice sounded again. Louder. Closer. "Matthias? Are you in the kitchen?"

Luke's brother stilled.

In a slow move, he turned around just as Lauren entered the room.

She stopped up short, her gaze jumping between their two faces. If she sensed the catastrophe in the offing, her expression didn't immediately show it. Instead, her hands tightened the sash of her robe, then she moved forward, her hand stretching for Matt's.

"Good morning," she said, her voice and smile warm.

Yeah, Luke thought, his body still in that frozen state. The looming catastrophe had yet to chill her air.

"It seems you've caught us," Lauren finished.

Oh, hell. She didn't have a clue.

Matt's hand stayed at his side and he just stared at her for a long, tense moment, taking in her short robe and the glimpse of thin nightgown underneath. Then his gaze shifted to Luke, wearing nothing but his pajama bottoms.

Finally, Matt laughed, a mirthless sound sharp enough to cut glass. "I guess I did catch you, didn't I? How long has this been going on? You and my brother, behind my back, f—"

"No." Before that ugliness could make it into the room, Luke's paralysis evaporated and he surged forward to slug his twin in the face. At the blow, his brother reeled back, Lauren shrieked, and the red tide rising in Luke's vision threatened to swamp him. He caught Matt by the shirt before he hit his head on the upper cabinets.

"Don't say that word," he snapped out, holding his brother steady. "That word is not what Lauren and I are about."

Matt's left eye was already swelling, though it didn't hinder its ferocious glitter. "That's not the way I see it," he said. "If there really is a 'Lauren and you,' then I've been royally—"

"Leave Lauren out of this," Luke broke in again, his voice harsh. "She didn't—she doesn't know it was me."

"What…what do you mean?" Lauren's voice. Lauren.

Luke watched his fists tighten on his brother's shirt. He couldn't turn his head and look at her. He couldn't speak another word.

"Damn it, lunkhead," Matt said, stepping back so he broke free of Luke's grasp. "What the hell have you done?"

What the hell *had* he done? It hit Luke, it hit him one brick at a time. Pretending to be his brother. For days and days. Making love to Lauren while she thought he was Matt. Time and time again.

Even with the engagement off the table, even when she'd said "can't we just be two people," it was still the most underhanded, ugly thing Luke had ever done in his life.

A something that, now, in the cold light of this morning, couldn't be excused, no matter what under-handed and ugly thing Matt had done or was trying to do to Luke's business.

Yes, Luke was the villain here. That destructive wolf he'd once imagined himself to be.

Swallowing hard, he forced himself to swing around, his gaze finding Goldilocks, her face pale and her blue eyes shadowed by growing suspicion.

"Lunkhead?" she echoed. "You—you said I didn't know it was you. What didn't I know? What's going on?"

And he had to put the pieces of the puzzle together for her—there were really three pieces, he realized now—as much as he wished they didn't fit. Three pieces: Matt, Lauren and himself.

"I'm Luke," he confessed. "I got a call, Matt wanted me take his month and, then…"

Lauren's hand rose to her throat. "He wanted you to take his fiancée, too?"

"Keep me out of this," Matt said, as he turned to pull a bag of frozen peas from the freezer. He winced as he placed it over his eye. "I was as much in the dark about my twin's little deception as you."

Lauren glanced over at Matt, then returned her gaze to Luke, horror overtaking the confusion on her face. "You…you were…"

A dozen excuses came to mind. Phrases that might, somehow, save the situation. Explanations that might, with luck or with charm or with both, absolve him. But his mouth refused to utter them. His lips would only form three words. "I was wrong."

They were the same three that sent her flying away from him.

In the master bedroom, Lauren worked at erasing her presence from Hunter's house. Maybe, just maybe, if she made it as if she'd never been here, then the past days would be like a dream—a nightmare—that she could wake from.

It didn't mean the monster wouldn't find her one last time, however. Though she'd hoped Matthias—no, *Luke*—would stay well clear of her after what he'd confessed in the kitchen, when she felt a little tingle at the base of her spine, she looked over to find the man who'd tricked her leaning against the doorjamb. Wrenching her gaze away from him, she continued stripping the sheets from the mattress.

"What are you doing?" he asked quietly.

With the bathroom towels in a pile on the floor and the pillowcases already on top of them, she thought he could figure it out. "Don't worry, I'll remake the bed," she said.

The tension in the room leaped higher and when she glanced over at him, she saw the new hard-set to his jaw. "Lauren…" he started, but then gusted out a sigh and stalked off.

She released her breath and rubbed her damp palms on her jeans. Maintaining her dignity while in his proximity was paramount—though next to impossible.

However, she wasn't going to leave until she completed this cathartic little process.

Or stall tactic. Maybe that's what it was. Because though she knew that Luke had betrayed her, it hadn't sunk in quite yet. At the moment she was almost numb…and she liked it that way.

The bottom sheet joined the pile of dirty linens. Then she turned toward the hallway to find clean ones but instead found him barring her exit from the bedroom, his arms full of what she was after.

"I'll take those," she said, sweeping them away.

Her gaze avoided his naked chest, even as the back of her hands tingled from where they'd rubbed against his. Without a word, he disappeared into the walk-in closet, but he was back too soon, now dressed in jeans and a T-shirt.

The Game Palace, it read. Where Guys Go To Get Game.

He'd played her, all right.

The thought jabbed through her anesthetized emotions and made a direct hit at her heart. Ducking her head, she reached deep for calm as she smoothed the bottom sheet along the mattress. It stretched away from her hands and she looked over to see Matthias— *Luke*—pulling it up to reach the opposite corner.

"I can do it myself," she hissed, then felt herself flush, embarrassed at the slip in her composure. *Find the numbness again,* she told herself. *Let him think it meant nothing to you. Let him think you don't care that you went to bed with the wrong man.*

Then how come it had felt so right?

She bit down hard on her bottom lip as she continued making up the bed. What was the big surprise that she'd messed up again? She'd been wrong three times before. The fourth should have been a given. It *had* been a given! She'd come here to Lake Tahoe to break it off, then she'd met Luke and he'd messed up her plans.

Her hands shook as she picked up a pillow. Then she found herself staring at him, across the width of the bed where they'd slept together so many nights. "Why did you do it?"

He shrugged, staring down at the fresh sheet before he looked up to meet her gaze again. "I told you once. I was tired of my brother having everything I want."

He hadn't wanted *her,* though. Not really. He'd merely wanted something of his brother's. She could see that now. "Were you laughing at me?"

His eyes closed. "No. Never." Then they opened, a faint smile trying to quirk the corners of his mouth. "Okay, sometimes, when you cried at those tragic movies."

"That's not funny, Matthias." She groaned at her own mistake, even as she felt hot tears sting the corner of her eyes. "Luke. *Luke.*"

She sank to the edge of the bed and rubbed her forehead with her hand. "Funny, in my mind I started thinking of you as the bad twin. I guess I was right."

"I guess you were," he agreed. "Because I can see now that my reasons—"

"You actually think you have an explanation for this?" Flabbergasted, she stared at him, then wiggled her fingers in a little go-ahead gesture. "I can't *wait* to hear it."

He scraped his hand over his face. "I told you about what happened with our father's will, how Matt cheated a supplier to make his million first."

"That's what you say happened."

"It's happening again now. I've been in talks with a company in Germany over the last few months, putting together something that's make-or-break for my company, Eagle Wireless. Everything seemed to be proceeding fine and dandy and when my brother asked me to do him the favor of taking his month at Hunter's house, I agreed. But then I found out the second day I was here that Matt was in Stuttgart, talking to my guy and trying to take over *my* deal."

And for a man like Luke who hated to lose… She knew all he didn't say, and it amazed her that he'd been able to hide his anger and frustration over the past few days. No wonder he'd found it so difficult to relax. Every minute with her here meant another minute jeopardizing the success of his company.

"But you have to see that this—" he continued, gesturing toward the half-made bed, "—you have to know that this was never something I did to hurt you."

"Well, you could never hurt me," she scoffed. She was numb, remember? Anesthetized. Thank God, because his brother's actions didn't excuse the way he'd used her. "I'm not hurt."

"The engagement—"

"I took that off the table, remember? *I* already broke up with *you*, if you'll recall. I'm not wearing your ring, right?" Then she looked down at her bare hand and laughed. "Oh, but that was Matthias's ring."

It struck her as funny now. So funny that she heard

herself laughing again as she thought of breaking up with Luke who wasn't Matthias. Of going to bed with the wrong brother who had felt so right. Of taking off Matthias's ring so Luke wouldn't feel bad about breaking his promise to her.

Of how she felt about the fiancé who wasn't her fiancé after all. Still laughing, she dropped her face to her hands and gave up any pretense of dignity. It was all too funny for that.

"Lauren?" Luke hurried around the bed and sat down beside her. "Are you okay?"

Her cheeks were wet with tears. "Don't you find it hysterical?" she managed to get out.

"What?" He lifted his hand as if he was going to touch her face, but then it fell to his thigh. "What's making you cry?"

"I'm laughing," she corrected him. It continued to bubble inside of her and she had to hold her palm over her stomach to hold it down. "I'm laughing, because for the first time in my failed career as a fiancée, I fell in love with the man who put a ring on my finger, only to find out he was still the wrong man after all."

She wiped her cheeks with the back of her hands. "Just like everyone else, you never really cared about me."

Too late she heard all that she'd revealed to him.

Too late she realized all the dignity she'd lost.

Too late she recalled almost the very first words he'd ever said to her: *Never show me your weakness, I'll use it against you.*

Luke found his brother in the kitchen, making another pot of coffee. Well, not making the coffee exactly. He had the ingredients at hand but he was frowning at the coffeemaker. The coffeemaker that had been perfectly fine earlier that morning but now had a malfunctioning readout that was blinking an angry red like a malevolent animal.

He shouldered Matt aside. "Let someone with tech savvy take over."

"Kendall always makes the coffee."

"Who?"

Matt dropped into a chair at the kitchen table. "Kendall, my assistant. She brings it to me, too."

Luke rolled his eyes. His assistant, Elaine, would throw the stapler at his head if he asked her to make him a coffee. His brother's actually delivered beverages. "One in a million," he murmured.

A kabillion.

His gut churned with bile. *A kabillion.* He remembered Lauren saying that, saying it was what they could make on their bottled sexual chemistry. Closing his eyes, he gripped the countertop and hung his head, waiting for the nausea to pass.

"So, where's my fiancée?" Matt asked, his voice casual.

His head whipped toward his brother. "She took off your ring."

Matt stretched his legs out in front of him. "When she thought you were me. I can understand that."

"Damn it, she came here to break off the engagement!"

Matt stifled a yawn behind his hand. "You didn't answer the question. Where's my fiancée?"

"She left, all right? She left—"

"You. She left you."

Luke was standing by the counter and the coffee-maker one minute. The next, he was jerking his brother out of his seat, holding him by fistfuls of his starched shirt. "She never wanted to marry you in the first place."

"What are you going to do about it, lunkhead? Give me another black eye? Is that the way you're solving your problems these days?"

Luke shoved Matt back in his chair. His brother's shiner was puffy and red and he didn't feel an ounce of guilt over it. "This is all your fault," he said. "Damn it, Matt, if you hadn't cheated me—"

"Aren't you sick of that song?" Matt rose from the chair, his voice tight. "I told you I didn't cheat you then, I told it to you earlier this morning, but I'm not going to tell you again. Damn it, I'm done with my part of this little tune."

He stalked toward the door, then paused for a long moment. With a tired shrug, he turned back around. "I came here to do the right thing. You took my place in the house as a favor. Do you need me to move in now so you can get back to work?"

I came here to do the right thing. Luke stared at his brother and then Lauren's voice sounded in his head— would he always hear her? *Neither of you would be satisfied to achieve victory through some sort of dirty trick.*

"Well?" Matt prompted. "Are you heading back to work?"

Work. Eagle Wireless. Luke ran his hand over his face. Back at the helm of his company, things would make sense again. There would be meetings, conference calls, engineers who need a butt kick in order to jump-start their latent skills in speaking non-tech English. Best of all, he could immediately board a plane for Stuttgart and do whatever it took to salvage his deal with Ernst.

With all that on his plate, he'd forget about his time here. He'd forget about Lauren. He'd forget about Matt's betrayal.

Neither of you would be satisfied to achieve victory through some sort of dirty trick.

His gaze lasered in on his brother. "Where've you been?"

"I told you when we spoke last week. Germany."

"Stuttgart? Ernst?"

His twin's good eye narrowed. "You know Ernst?"

Luke laughed. So much for brotherhood. "He's *my* guy, as if you didn't know."

A strange expression crossed Matt's face. "What?"

"You must know I've been working on him to make a deal with Eagle Wireless. So I'm guessing you have a spy in my company. Somebody else you're paying off to your advantage."

"I don't have anyone I'm paying off in your company," Matt retorted, but then his voice slowed. "That I know of."

Luke laughed again. But as that odd expression once more crossed his brother's face, he swallowed his scorn.

Neither of you would be satisfied to achieve victory through some sort of dirty trick.

Luke shoved his hand through his hair. "Look, I've been in contact with Ernst since last fall. When did you hear about him?"

"Fall? I've only been talking to Ernst this last month." Matt looked off, his jaw tightening just as Luke's did when he was angry. "Hell."

"Damn it, Matt," Luke said. "Tell me you didn't cheat me seven years ago."

His brother's one-eyed gaze jerked back to his face. "I've told you and told you."

"Just tell me again." Luke grabbed up a few of the photos spread on the table, his gut churning once more as he felt poised on the brink of something big. Something really, really big.

"Here in Hunter's house, swear on the brothers we used to be." He held out the evidence toward his twin.

Matt reached out for the photos, but he didn't look away from Luke's face. "I'd rather chew off my own arm than admit this, Luke, but what you said about Ernst means I have to investigate what's going on. Someone I've trusted may have conned us both out of quite a lot. Believe me, though, on the memory of our good friend Hunter Palmer, on the memory of the kind of brothers we used to be, I didn't knowingly cheat you. I swear."

In a decisive strike, those last two words blew a hole in Luke's defensive wall of bitter anger. Emotions long-dammed up released, pouring relief, sadness and a weird kind of elation into his bloodstream. His brother hadn't cheated him.

He had his brother back.

"Matt." Though he felt dizzy with the revelation, he could breathe easier, he found. After all these years, he could finally take a deep breath. "I believe you, Matt."

A faint smile turned up his brother's mouth. "Say 'I believe you, meathead.'"

Meathead and lunkhead. The names from their childhood when the enemy had been each other.

"He still wouldn't be sorry for what he did to us," Luke said.

Matt knew exactly who he was talking about. Exactly what he was talking about. "Dear old Dad and those destructive games he made us play."

"I hope we can get past him, and them, again." Luke looked at the photos his brother still held. "We did in college."

"You slept with my fiancée."

Lauren. Oh, God, Lauren.

With the emotional dam that had been inside of him now destroyed, there was no longer any protection against the guilt and remorse now coursing through him like a flood. He'd hurt Lauren.

Lauren, who was in love with him.

Lauren, who'd said, *Just like everyone else, you never really cared about me.*

But Luke did care about her. Luke cared a whole hell of a lot, and he couldn't let her go on with her life thinking he was yet another failed fiancé. Except that failed fiancé would be Matt, wouldn't it?

And that made him feel better, even as it struck him again what an arrogant, unfeeling bastard he'd been, using Lauren to get back at his brother.

I'm in love with you. She'd said that.

And he'd broken her heart.

But it would be all right, wouldn't it? Give her a

couple of days and she'd realize his sorry soul wasn't worth her smiles, her laughter, her touch, her heart.

Hell.

He couldn't live with that.

"You're staying here at the house," he told his brother, making a swift decision. "I have somewhere I've got to be."

"Some*one* you've got to *see?*" Matt asked, lifting the bag of frozen peas to his face again.

"You don't love her." As a twin, he knew he was speaking the truth.

"I don't love her," Matt admitted, removing the plastic to gaze at him with both eyes. "But I was talking about Ernst."

"Ernst?" Already Luke had forgotten about flying to Germany. He waved the man's name away. "It's Lauren I'm thinking about." Lauren, who he'd betrayed.

Matt shook his head and replaced the bag of peas. "What makes you think she's going to be happy to see you?"

Luke refused to be defeated by the idea. "I'll make it right with her," he told his brother. He had to. "No matter what. It's the Barton family motto, remember? Assume success, deny failure."

Matt shrugged. "All right. Maybe it'll be okay. Maybe you just need to get your foot in the door."

Luke's shoulders sagged. She wouldn't let him get his foot in the door, would she? By the time she drove home, he was certain she would have convinced herself she never wanted to see him again.

If Luke showed up she wouldn't let him get within twenty feet.

But what if…?

He looked at his brother. "There's something else you have to do for me," he said to Matt. "And I think you're going to like it."

Ten

Dinner hour, *casa* Conover. Lauren looked around the table at her little sister, her mother and then her father who had just seated himself after making them wait while he finished a phone call. Though she'd only been back in the family house a mere twenty-four hours, it was as if she'd never left.

"That bumbling Bilbray," her father muttered as their housekeeper, June, set his steaming plate of chicken Kiev in front of him. "It's as if he doesn't understand the law of supply and demand. Didn't he go to business school? Hasn't he been working for me for more than fifteen years? Do I have to teach him to tie his shoes as well as read a spreadsheet?"

Lauren turned to her sister, raising her voice over her father's continued annoyed ramblings. "What were you saying, Kaitlyn? That Mr. Beall wants to you to design the drama department's page on the school Web site?"

Without waiting for an answer, she swiveled toward her father. "Dad, did you hear that? Kaitlyn's drama teacher is going to be paying her real money for Web site design."

At the word *money* her father paused in his brain-less Bilbray-litany and glanced in his younger daughter's direction. "We could use the extra cash now that Lauren's broken it off with Matthias Barton. Though maybe I can do something about that. Maybe I can give that young man a call and—"

"Dad," Lauren interrupted. "I don't want to marry Matthias Barton."

"He'll probably give you another chance, you know. He's as eager to be aligned with Conover Industries as we are eager to be aligned with him, and—"

"Dad, I'm not going to marry Matthias Barton."

Lauren's mother looked up from her chicken Kiev, a spark lighting in her eyes. "Ralph, do you really think you can persuade Matthias to reconsider Lauren? Despite her rash response to another of her Bad Ideas? I haven't had a chance to cancel the reservations for the reception yet—"

"What?" Lauren stared at her mother. "You didn't tell me you'd booked a venue for the reception. We hadn't even started talking about that yet."

Carole Conover waved her manicured fingers. "I've had my eye on this particular Napa winery for years. You could have the wedding there, too, if you'd like, though maybe Matthias would prefer a church service instead."

Lauren shook her head in disbelief. "By all means, let's consult Matthias," she muttered to herself.

Kaitlyn's voice piped up from across the table. "There *was* that pretty junior bridesmaid's dress. I could live with the blue one with the ribbon sash."

Lauren's gaze jumped toward her sister. *"Et tu?"*

Their mother beamed at Kaitlyn. "I think you're right. Definitely the blue one with the sash."

Lauren wanted to scream. She wanted to rent her clothes. She wanted to find a completely unsuitable groom and elope to Lithuania. Ha, she thought. *Maybe Trevor can be convinced to leave his ski-heiress for me. Then* her parents would be sorry.

Which was exactly why she'd agreed to marry Trevor the first time, she realized. And why she'd said yes to her father's mechanic. And why it had almost been oui with Jean-Paul on the top of the Eiffel Tower. Luke had suggested that to her, hadn't he? And now she saw it, too. All her previous fiancés had been perfect-perfect paragons of parental rebellion.

Oh God. Had she really tried standing up to her overbearing mother and father by marrying the wrong man time and again?

And again?

Good God. If that was true, bumbling Bilbray was way more on the ball than Lauren.

"How shall you handle this, Ralph?" her mother was saying. "Maybe keep it simple and tell Matthias Barton that Lauren was just suffering a little case of cold feet?"

During which she'd slept with your brother and fallen in love with the jerk, Lauren finished for her mother. Not that she'd shared with her parents that part of her Tahoe visit. Maybe they'd been right all along. Maybe she had no business deciding what to do with her own life because she just kept on botching it up.

"I've always thought September weddings were special," her mother said with a sigh. "It's a lovely time of year for a honeymoon."

Lauren grimaced. No matter what, no matter who, it wasn't happening in September. "I'm committed to a conference for the publishing house that month, Mom. There's not room for anything else on my calendar then."

Her father waved away her objection with his fork. "Nonsense. You can just quit that silly job if it gets in the way of your wedding."

"Silly job?" Lauren echoed, even as her father went back to his meal. "Dad, I make a good living as a translator. I could even take my skills and help you out at Conover if you'd let me."

"Help me out how?"

"Translating, Dad. You know, what I've been trained for? What I've been doing for several years now. I even have a hefty bank balance to prove it. Other companies besides the publisher pay me tidy sums for my work involving technological and business matters. It's not easy to find people who can not only translate, but translate techno-speak as well."

Her father started to bluster. "We have a company on retainer—"

"Linguanotics. I know them. I know Jeremy Cloud, who does most of their work for you. I'm better. And I'd like to put together a presentation that will show you just how and why you should hire me as a consultant instead. I guarantee you won't be sorry."

Her entire family was staring at her in surprise. Lauren herself felt energized, focused, her senses as honed as when she competed against her arch-nemesis, Luke. This was what it felt like to tackle things head-on with an intention to win, she realized.

And she liked it. It was the one good thing she could lay at Luke's door—that he'd taught her the power there was in assuming success and denying failure.

"Well...I—I—" Her father sputtered, looking over at her mother for help.

"I'm sure your father will give you time for a presentation," Carole said smoothly. "But why don't you wait until after the honeymoon, all right?"

It was straightforward straight talk time once again. Lauren's heart sped up as she gripped the edge of the table and leaned toward her mother. "Mom, you need to listen to me. I'm not going to marry that man. There isn't going to be a wedding in September. Cancel the winery, call off the dressmaker, rip up any other plans you've been hatching behind my back."

"Lauren—"

"There's going to be no wedding," Lauren interjected, her voice firm. "I'm not going to marry Matthias and he certainly doesn't want to marry me."

The sound of a throat clearing had everyone swiveling in their seat. June stood on the threshold to the dining room, clutching the skirt of her apron in her hands. Her face was flushed. "Um...there's someone here."

"Someone who?" her father demanded, his gaze

flicking to the grandfather clock in the corner of the room.

"Mr. Matthias Barton."

Lauren groaned as her mother shot her a triumphant look.

Luke was practically choking thanks to his Matt-tight tie as he was shown into the Conover dining room by the pink-cheeked housekeeper. The first person his gaze landed on was a young girl—Kaitlyn, of course—and he sent her a little grin as she reacted to his face with a wince.

Then *he* winced a little, too, because the smile hurt like hell.

"Barton!" Ralph Conover stood up from his place at the table and reached out his hand. "Have you had dinner?"

Luke hadn't seen the older man in years, but even if he hadn't already recognized him he would have known him by the Lauren-blue of his eyes. "I'm fine, sir, no dinner for me. I'm sorry to disturb you, but I came to see if I might have a word with your older daughter."

He sent her a sidelong glance, but she was staring down at her plate, as if mesmerized by her asparagus.

"Lauren?" her mother prompted. "Why don't you and Matthias go have a nice long chat in the library?"

A moment passed, then, with a resigned nod, the younger woman pushed back her chair. As they exited the room, Kaitlyn called out, "Don't forget the blue dress, Lauren. It's really pretty."

In the library, she shut the double doors behind them, then spoke without facing him. "I left the engagement ring on the dresser in the master bedroom," she said. "I should have told you that before I left. Now, if there's nothing else…"

Luke stared as she started turning the double door-knobs again. She was leaving the room? Leaving his life? "Wait…wait…"

She spun to face him. "What? What is it you want, Matthias?"

He was stupid. He'd had hours with which to figure out what to say right now, and he'd thought of nothing beyond finding a way to be alone with her again. "About my brother…"

"That's quite a shiner he gave you."

"Yeah." Matt hadn't been as reluctant as Luke might have wished to give him a matching punch to the face. But he'd realized he deserved it and more for what he'd done. Most important, he'd been certain that Lauren wouldn't have agreed to see him as himself, Luke.

So he'd gone for the ole twin switcheroo again. Maybe he should feel more guilt over that, but at the moment there was only desperation in his heart.

"Look," he started, still hoping for inspiration to strike. "My brother, he's really sorry—"

"About being as stupid as I was in agreeing to marry a near-perfect stranger?"

"He can be a little single-minded about business, too, and he thought—" Luke broke off, realizing what she'd said. Realizing that she'd seen through the switcheroo. "So you know."

"Fool me once, shame on you," she said, her face expressionless. "Fool me twice, shame on me. What are you out for now, Luke? More revenge?"

His face ached like a hammered thumb and it was all for nothing, damn it. And the pain was making it hard to think. "I wanted to try again to explain what happened."

She crossed her arms over her chest. "Your brother stole something from you and you wanted to steal something from him. I get that."

Luke shook his head. "That thing with Matt…we don't know what happened exactly, only that it was something shady, but I now know he didn't do it to me."

For a moment her stony face softened. "Oh, Luke. You have your twin again."

"Yeah. Maybe. I'm hopeful." His hand went to the egg on the back of his skull. "Though he's gained a powerful punch over the last few years. When he hit me I fell back and cracked my head on the table. I was seeing double from my one good eye until noon, which is why it took me an extra day to get here."

If he thought she might respond to the sympathy card, he was wrong. Her face was cold again and that's how he felt, too, cold with…with…hell, he had to admit it. Cold with fear.

What if he couldn't get through to her?

"But someone robbed something from me, after all," he blurted out.

"I told you where the ring is."

"That's Matt's, and you know I'm not interested in a damn piece of jewelry." The cold inside of him was as icy as the blue of her eyes, and it was slowing his heartbeat to a death knell.

How could he go on without her beside him? Who would he have to watch sappy movies with? Who would give him a pinch when he was getting too competitive?

After Hunter had died, there had been no one to show him the wider, brighter world until Lauren. Even if Matt had his back, who would be at his side?

It had to be Lauren. He only wanted Lauren.

He was in love with Lauren.

The thought ran like a flame through cold snow. Until this moment, he'd never allowed himself to even silently form the words, now he was consumed by them. He was in love with his Goldilocks, with her humor and her sweet disposition. With her knack for relaxing and the way the air heated when they were in a room together.

He was in love with her blond hair and her curvy body, from her short nose to her short toes, and every inch of creamy skin in between. He loved her full breasts and her pink nipples. He loved the almost transparent color of the curls that did little to protect her sex from his gaze. He loved the little sounds she made when he touched her there and found her already wet and her little bud—

"Luke."

From her annoyed expression and flushed cheeks, he figured she'd read just about all of that on his face.

"Luke, why did you come here?"

He squashed his panic at her cold, angry tone. She wasn't just falling into his arms as he might have hoped, but that didn't mean he'd give up. Bartons never gave up, and he sent out a silent prayer of thanks to his father for that. Amazing, that loving Lauren could even give him a new appreciation of Samuel Sullivan Barton.

"Luke—"

"You did take something of mine." The words tumbled out.

Her brows came together in a frown. "What?"

Here it was. Time to hand over the power. In business, he'd taught himself to always hold back, to keep some of his cards to himself, but now…now if he really wanted her he would have to lay it all on the table. He'd never had much faith in loyalty, but now he was going to have to take the risk and believe that this woman would give him hers.

"I don't want back what you took, though," he said, stalling. "You can keep it. You can have it forever."

Her frown deepened. "Well, what is it?"

Here goes. "My heart."

Lauren remembered the time she'd told Luke he looked as if she'd hit him with a cartoon frying pan, and she was certain that was the same expression she wore now. It certainly felt as if something had struck her, knocking the breath straight out of her lungs. "Wh-what?"

"I don't know if you took my heart or if I gave it or when it happened or how I could get so lucky. Maybe it's like Kaitlyn's rule and that true…true beauty only comes upon us by surprise. I wasn't expecting this, Lauren, but with you I see things so much clearer. I have a perspective that I've been missing nearly all my life. With you, I can think about breathing instead of about winning. With you, I can forget about my business and the constant hustle to make the next buck."

It was the longest speech she'd ever heard him make.

His voice, a little hoarse, a little breathless, rang with sincerity. Shaking her head, she flattened her hands against the creamy white paint of the doors and stared at him, trying to understand. Luke's eyes were serious, their expression intent.

Again, sincere.

But…but…

"You…your brother…you always want what he has," she reminded them both. "Now you're only trying to get back at him for that Stuttgart thing."

"This isn't about Matt anymore, Lauren," Luke said. "Please, please believe me, though I know I don't deserve your trust."

He *didn't* deserve her trust! "You seduced me under false pretences."

"Yes."

"You came here today, doing the same all over again."

He grimaced. "Yes. And I'm sorry, so sorry. Not so much about today, though. I needed to do whatever it took to see you again. To try to explain—"

"You shouldn't have bothered," Lauren said, bitterness giving bite to her words. "While it might be difficult for me to forgive you, believe me, I understand. I'm Ralph Conover's daughter, remember? I'm accustomed to the lengths a man will go for his business."

Her father's single-mindedness had been something she'd always half-joked about, but it had rankled her entire life. Even more as she grew older and saw how it affected Kaitlyn. The whole family had lost out on so much during his ruthless drive for the all-mighty dollar.

After the way Luke was raised, it was no surprise he was filled with the same competitive, cold-hearted zeal.

"So go away," she said, turning her face so she could avoid his. "Get on the first flight to Stuttgart and beat out your brother that way."

There was a long moment of silence, then Luke spoke again. "Lauren." It sounded strained. "Lauren, please look at me."

That was a mistake. Because despite his competitive, cold-hearted zeal, he had the appearance of a man who was more worried about losing than consumed with winning.

"I could *be* in Stuttgart right now if that's what was important to me," he said. "Matt's at Hunter's house to fulfill the stipulation of the will and if I wanted I could be in Europe, working on Ernst. *Without* a hell of a shiner, I might add, and without a bump on the back of my head bigger than a baseball. I didn't go to Stuttgart. I came to you."

Her heart jolted, one hard thump against her ribs. For the second time her breath was knocked right out of her.

Luke hadn't gone to Stuttgart.

He hadn't left Hunter's house at the first instant he could to shore up his business deal.

How could this be? How could competitive, cut-throat, cold-hearted Luke have abandoned the most important thing to him in the world?

She said it out loud, just to be sure. "You didn't go to Stuttgart." Her voice came out a whisper.

"I haven't given Germany another thought since you walked out on me," he replied. "I didn't go to Stuttgart because I wanted to be with you. I want to be with you because when we're together I actually enjoy the life that Hunter is no longer here to share. I finally figured out why he arranged that situation for the Samurai— or at least why he arranged it for me. I needed to reconnect with people again, Lauren. I needed to realize that I'm actually one myself, a person with emotions, and needs, and fears…and…and love. I'm so in love with you."

He was in love with her! Lauren felt her stomach fall toward her knees. He was in love with her? Before, he'd said she had his heart, but she'd still been trying to convince herself he didn't have one. But to say this, to say he was in love with her. And to give up his important business deal so that he could…

It was true. It must be true.

Oh, Luke.

She took a slow step forward. He froze, just watching her with those serious, worried eyes, as if afraid to believe what he was seeing.

She remembered dozens of sweet hours in his arms. Dozens of conversations about movies, travel, nothing at all. It hadn't mattered one wit what he called himself. It was the man, and not the name, she'd fallen for. Taking another forward step, she remembered again the exact moment she'd realized it, when he'd been angry, for her, at Trevor.

Her forward movement halted, her feet digging into the carpet.

Luke must have read the renewed reluctance on her face. For a second his eyes closed as if he experienced a sharp pain. Then they opened, and she could see that pain in his eyes.

Tears stung hers.

"What is it, Goldilocks? What's coming between you and my arms?" The tightness of his voice showed his strain. "I love you. Don't you believe me? Don't you believe that the man who was with you at Hunter's house, whether his name was Matt or Luke, was a man who fell in love with you?"

She shook her head, mute. That Luke hadn't hurried off to Stuttgart proved the strength of his feelings. The problem, at the moment, wasn't him.

"What can I do?" he asked, hoarser now. "What can I do to make you mine? I want to marry you, Lauren."

"I'm afraid," she said. Thinking of Trevor had opened the door to it. "I've been engaged three times before. Each time the decision was wrong."

"Make that four times, sweetheart." Luke grimaced. "Remember? I'm not Matt."

Her eyes widened and she felt them sting again. "You're right. Four mistakes. Luke…"

His hands fisted at his sides. She could see him holding himself back. Luke would always be one who reacted with action, whose first instinct would be to take matters into his own hands and force the results he wanted. But here he was, letting her come to her own conclusions. It made her love him more…feel even more unsure of what she should do about it.

"Lauren, sweetheart." He blew out a breath. "Trust yourself."

"*Myself?* Trust *myself?* What kind of reasoning is that? I'm the one who picked Trevor and Joe and Jean-Paul."

"You know what I think about them? I think you picked those three with your parents in mind, and if

that's the case, then they were exactly the wrong men—
which was exactly right for what you were after at the
time."

Oh, God. That was true. Hadn't she acknowledged
it during dinner? They'd been perfect men for her
perfect parental rebellion. Luke knew her so well. And
yet still loved her. How could she turn away from that?
Four fiancés should have taught her *something*.

"This time, Goldilocks, if I might make a suggestion,
why don't you pick the man who is just right for you."

Lauren loved the library. As a little girl, she used to
tuck herself away behind one of the leather wing chairs
and pour over old atlases that listed exotically named
countries such as Persia and Wallachia and Travan-
core. She dreamed of the people who lived there and
the sounds of their spoken languages.

Later, she dreamed of visiting those places with a
man who would share her curiosity and who would
make her spin with dizzy happiness—like the globe
sitting on the table in front of the mullioned windows.

Of course, she'd never imagined she'd be cradling
her love's head on her lap while applying a bag of
petite white corn kernels to his battered face—but she
crooned sympathetically to him in French and Spanish
as a way of making up for it.

He opened his good eye. "Did you just call me a little
toad?"

"Only because of all these new lumps on your skull,"
she said, trying not to laugh. Laughter jostled her legs
which in turn put pressure on the bump on the back of
his head. "Are you sure you shouldn't see a doctor?"

"Your mother won't let me out of the house, not now that we've convinced her *our* engagement isn't a big hoax to get back at her for not taking your career seriously."

"Thank you for making that point to her when she started going off on a September wedding date again. I'm determined to manage her in just such a straightforward manner from now on." Lauren leaned down to press her mouth lightly to his.

When he tried to take the kiss deeper, she pulled back. "No. You're supposed to be resting."

His eye closed and his lips curved up in a smile. "We'll go back to Hunter's house tomorrow and rest up for the remainder of my month."

"I'm a little afraid to let you go to sleep, though," Lauren said. Her gaze traveled over the face that had become the map to her happiness. "What if, thanks to that bump on your head, when you wake up you don't remember me?"

He opened his good eye again and the expression she read there made the love inside of her expand until there wasn't room for breath.

"Then we'll become acquainted all over again, Goldilocks, because the Big Bad Wolf has finally caught the pretty girl—and he isn't ever letting her go."

Lauren and Luke were making a final walk-through of Hunter's house before they left it for the last time. She peered under the bed and spotted a penny on the carpet in the very middle—too far to reach even if she got down on her hands and knees.

With a little smile to herself, she left it where it lay.

Maybe the coin would bring the next Samurai the same good luck Luke swore he'd found here.

On her last sweep of the master bathroom, she discovered a note taped to the mirror. Luke's handwriting was as dark and aggressive as he was, and, no surprise, he didn't waste time with greetings or goodbyes. It only read:

> Dev: Remember the talk we had about women on New Year's Eve our senior year? We were wrong, man. So wrong. We didn't have a clue.

Luke came up behind her as she read over the words. She looked up to meet his gaze in the glass. "Well?" she asked.

His lips twitched. "Well, what?"

"What's it mean? What didn't you two have a clue about?"

Tenderness replaced amusement in his eyes. He twirled a curl of her hair around his finger. "You'll meet Devlin Campbell someday very soon, Goldilocks. And then you can ask him."

* * * * *

The MILLIONAIRE OF THE MONTH
series continues with Susan Crosby's
BOUND BY THE BABY,
available May 2007 from Silhouette Desire.

Set in darkness beyond the ordinary world.
Passionate tales of life and death.
With characters' lives ruled by laws the everyday
world can't begin to imagine.

n●cturne

It's time to discover the Raintree trilogy...

New York Times bestselling author
LINDA HOWARD
brings you the dramatic first book
RAINTREE: INFERNO

The Ansara Wizards are rising and the Raintree clan
must rejoin the battle against their foes, testing their
powers, relationships and forcing upon them lives
they never could have imagined before...

Turn the page for a sneak preview
of the captivating first book
in the Raintree trilogy,
RAINTREE: INFERNO by LINDA HOWARD
On sale April 25.

Dante Raintree stood with his arms crossed as he watched the woman on the monitor. The image was in black and white to better show details; color distracted the brain. He focused on her hands, watching every move she made, but what struck him most was how uncommonly *still* she was. She didn't fidget or play with her chips, or look around at the other players. She peeked once at her down card, then didn't touch it again, signaling for another hit by tapping a fingernail on the table. Just because she didn't seem to be paying attention to the other players, though, didn't mean she was as unaware as she seemed.

"What's her name?" Dante asked.

"Lorna Clay," replied his chief of security, Al Rayburn.

"At first I thought she was counting, but she doesn't pay enough attention."

"She's paying attention, all right," Dante murmured. "You just don't see her doing it." A card counter had to remember every card played. Supposedly counting cards was impossible with the number of decks used by the casinos, but there were those rare individuals who could calculate the odds even with multiple decks.

"I thought that, too," said Al. "But look at this piece of tape coming up. Someone she knows comes up to her and speaks, she looks around and starts chatting, completely misses the play of the people to her left—and doesn't look around even when the deal comes back to her, just taps that finger. And damn if she didn't win. Again."

Dante watched the tape, rewound it, watched it again. Then he watched it a third time. There had to be something he was missing, because he couldn't pick out a single giveaway.

"If she's cheating," Al said with something like respect, "she's the best I've ever seen."

"What does your gut say?"

Al scratched the side of his jaw, considering. Finally, he said, "If she isn't cheating, she's the luckiest person walking. She wins. Week in, week out, she wins. Never a huge amount, but I ran the numbers and she's into us for about five grand a week. Hell, boss, on her way out of the casino she'll stop by a slot machine, feed a dollar in and walk away with at least fifty. It's never the same machine, either. I've had her watched, I've had her followed, I've even looked for the same faces in the casino every time she's in here, and I can't find a common denominator."

"Is she here now?"

"She came in about half an hour ago. She's playing blackjack, as usual."

"Bring her to my office," Dante said, making a swift decision. "Don't make a scene."

"Got it," said Al, turning on his heel and leaving the security center.

Dante left, too, going up to his office. His face was calm. Normally he would leave it to Al to deal with a cheater, but he was curious. How was she doing it? There were a lot of bad cheaters, a few good ones, and every so often one would come along who was the stuff of which legends were made: the cheater who didn't get caught, even when people were alert and the camera was on him—or, in this case, her.

It was possible to simply be lucky, as most people understood luck. Chance could turn a habitual loser into a big-time winner. Casinos, in fact, thrived on that hope. But luck itself wasn't habitual, and he knew that what passed for luck was often something else: cheating. And there was the other kind of luck, the kind he himself possessed, but it depended not on chance but on who and what he was. He knew it was an innate power and not Dame Fortune's erratic smile. Since power like his was rare, the odds made it likely the woman he'd been watching was merely a very clever cheat.

Her skill could provide her with a very good living, he thought, doing some swift calculations in his head. Five grand a week equaled $260,000 a year, and that was just from his casino. She probably hit them all, careful to keep the numbers relatively low so she stayed under the radar.

He wondered how long she'd been taking him, how long she'd been winning a little here, a little there, before Al noticed.

The curtains were open on the wall-to-wall window in his office, giving the impression, when one first opened the door, of stepping out onto a covered balcony. The glazed window faced west, so he could catch the sunsets. The sun was low now, the sky painted in purple and gold. At his home in the mountains, most of the windows faced east, affording him views of the sunrise. Something in him needed both the greeting and the goodbye of the sun. He'd always been drawn to sunlight, maybe because fire was his element to call, to control.

He checked his internal time: four minutes until sundown. Without checking the sunrise tables every day, he knew exactly when the sun would slide behind the mountains. He didn't own an alarm clock. He didn't need one. He was so acutely attuned to the sun's position that he had only to check within himself to know the time. As for waking at a particular time, he was one of those people who could tell himself to wake at a certain time, and he did. That talent had nothing to do with being Raintree, so he didn't have to hide it; a lot of perfectly ordinary people had the same ability.

He had other talents and abilities, however, that did require careful shielding. The long days of summer in- stilled in him an almost sexual high, when he could feel contained power buzzing just beneath his skin. He had to be doubly careful not to cause candles to leap into flame just by his presence, or to start wildfires with a glance in the dry-as-tinder brush. He loved Reno; he didn't want to burn it down. He just felt so damn *alive* with all the sunshine pouring down that he wanted to let the energy pour through him instead of holding it inside.

This must be how his brother Gideon felt while pulling lightning, all that hot power searing through his muscles, his veins. They had this in common, the connection with raw power. All the members of the far-flung Raintree clan had some power, some heightened ability, but only members of the royal family could channel and control the earth's natural energies.

Dante wasn't just of the royal family, he was the Dranir, the leader of the entire clan. "Dranir" was synonymous with king, but the position he held wasn't ceremonial, it was one of sheer power. He was the oldest son of the previous Dranir, but he would have been passed over for the position if he hadn't also inherited the power to hold it.

Behind him came Al's distinctive knock on the door. The outer office was empty, Dante's secretary having gone home hours before. "Come in," he called, not turning from his view of the sunset.

The door opened, and Al said, "Mr. Raintree, this is Lorna Clay."

Dante turned and looked at the woman, all his senses on alert. The first thing he noticed was the vibrant color of her hair, a rich, dark red that encompassed a multitude of shades from copper to burgundy. The warm amber light danced along the iridescent strands, and he felt a hard tug of sheer lust in his gut. Looking at her hair was almost like looking at fire, and he had the same reaction.

The second thing he noticed was that she was spitting mad.

nocturne™

IT'S TIME TO DISCOVER
THE RAINTREE TRILOGY...

There have always been those among us
who are more than human...

Don't miss the dramatic first book by
New York Times bestselling author

LINDA
HOWARD

RAINTREE:
Inferno

On sale May.

Raintree: Haunted by Linda Winstead Jones
Available June.

Raintree: Sanctuary by Beverly Barton
Available July.

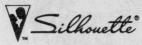

Silhouette®

Romantic
SUSPENSE

Sparked *by* **Danger,**
Fueled *by* **Passion.**

This month and every month look for
four new heart-racing romances
set against a backdrop of suspense!

Available in May 2007

Safety in Numbers
(Wild West Bodyguards miniseries)
by **Carla Cassidy**

Jackson's Woman
by **Maggie Price**

Shadow Warrior
(Night Guardians miniseries)
by **Linda Conrad**

One Cool Lawman
by **Diane Pershing**

Available wherever you buy books!

Visit Silhouette Books at www.eHarlequin.com   SRS0407

REQUEST YOUR FREE BOOKS!

2 FREE NOVELS PLUS 2 FREE GIFTS!

Silhouette® Desire®

Passionate, Powerful, Provocative!

YES! Please send me 2 FREE Silhouette Desire® novels and my 2 FREE gifts. After receiving them, if I don't wish to receive any more books, I can return the shipping statement marked "cancel." If I don't cancel, I will receive 6 brand-new novels every month and be billed just $3.80 per book in the U.S., or $4.47 per book in Canada, plus 25¢ shipping and handling per book and applicable taxes, if any*. That's a savings of almost 15% off the cover price! I understand that accepting the 2 free books and gifts places me under no obligation to buy anything. I can always return a shipment and cancel at any time. Even if I never buy another book from Silhouette, the two free books and gifts are mine to keep forever.

225 SDN EEXJ 326 SDN EEXU

Name	(PLEASE PRINT)	
Address		Apt.
City	State/Prov.	Zip/Postal Code

Signature (if under 18, a parent or guardian must sign)

Mail to the Silhouette Reader Service™:
IN U.S.A.: P.O. Box 1867, Buffalo, NY 14240-1867
IN CANADA: P.O. Box 609, Fort Erie, Ontario L2A 5X3

Not valid to current Silhouette Desire subscribers.

Want to try two free books from another line?
Call 1-800-873-8635 or visit www.morefreebooks.com.

* Terms and prices subject to change without notice. NY residents add applicable sales tax. Canadian residents will be charged applicable provincial taxes and GST. This offer is limited to one order per household. All orders subject to approval. Credit or debit balances in a customer's account(s) may be offset by any other outstanding balance owed by or to the customer. Please allow 4 to 6 weeks for delivery.

Your Privacy: Silhouette is committed to protecting your privacy. Our Privacy Policy is available online at www.eHarlequin.com or upon request from the Reader Service. From time to time we make our lists of customers available to reputable firms who may have a product or service of interest to you. If you would prefer we not share your name and address, please check here. ☐

SDES07

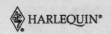